FISHERMAN
JACK

For Frances
    and Matthew

FISHERMAN JACK

MARY ST. HELIER

LUTTERWORTH PRESS

GUILDFORD SURREY ENGLAND

First Paperback edition 1969
Reprinted 1977
Reprinted 1982

This paperback edition copyright © 1969 by Lutterworth Press

ISBN 0 7188 1591 2

Printed in Great Britain
by Fletcher & Son Ltd, Norwich

CONTENTS

Chapter 1

JACK AT HOME

JACK GODDEN sat at the table eating his porridge. His baby sister Nellie lay and chuckled in her cradle, and their mother gave her a crust of bread to chew. Baby Nellie had five teeth, and Jack was very proud of her, and would have given her bits of his own breakfast if his mother had allowed it; but somehow she preferred to see to Baby's food herself ever since she found Jack giving the child a piece of kipper. Jack thought his mother made rather a fuss on that occasion, but as she was not the sort of mother who made fusses all the time, he decided that there must be something about babies and kippers that did not go together, and respected her wishes in the matter.

Now, as he ate his porridge, he noticed that she often looked restlessly out of the window, and once went to the open door and stared down the road.

"What's the matter, Mum"? he asked.

"Your dad's not in yet", she answered.

Jack stared in astonishment.

"What—didn't he come home last night"? he exclaimed. "I thought he was in bed and asleep. I wouldn't have been so quiet coming downstairs if I hadn't thought he was in bed."

"No, he didn't come in", said Mrs. Godden

absently. She went to the door again and looked out, then returned to her seat at the table with a sigh. "Get on with your breakfast, Jack. He'll come; there's no sense worrying."

Jack was not very much inclined to worry, and pushed aside his empty porridge-plate and seized a big piece of bread and dripping. His father had been late home before, and it never occurred to him that anything might go wrong. He adored his father and thought him the cleverest fisherman in Hythe, and his happiest moments were the rare occasions when he was allowed to go out fishing at night with him. Mum did not often allow it, and certainly never during school time, but it sometimes happened during the holidays that Dad said, "Get your sou'wester and sea-boots, son; you're coming out with us to-night." And then Jack would feel that he was the happiest boy in all the world.

The Goddens lived in a little cottage in Sandgate Lane, a short road that led from the canal to the sea front. At the end of the road were big houses, hotels and cafés, but if you turned to the right you came to the place where the fishing-boats were drawn up on to the beach, where ropes were coiled and nets were drying, and where Jack and his friend Tony Brew spent many a happy hour playing at being fishermen.

The Brews lived next door to the Goddens, and Arthur Brew was Ben Godden's partner in the boat *Mary Uden*. Jack's father, Ben Godden, had called the boat after his wife, for her name had been Mary Uden before she married him and became Mrs. Godden. Jack though it was a very good name for a boat, and he liked the fancy way it was painted on the side, too. His father had got a man to come out from the town to do it, and it had cost a lot of money, so he had been told. Jack was sure that the *Mary Uden* was the finest boat on the beach.

He also thought that Tony Brew was the finest pal a chap could have. The two of them did everything together. Tony had a sister, Betty, and she usually went with them everywhere. Sometimes Mrs. Brew thought that Betty ought to help her with the beds, or with the washing-up, but she was never there when wanted.

"Out with those dratted boys, I suppose," Mrs. Brew would grumble, and of course she was right.

It sometimes crossed Jack's mind that Tony and Betty were a bit unlucky in their parents. At any rate, he was sure Mr. and Mrs. Brew were not as nice as his own father and mother. Tony was inclined to be of that opinion too, but Betty scolded them furiously if she caught them discussing their parents. She said it was wicked and Tony must not do it, but Tony would catch Jack's eye and wink, and then they would talk about something else.

The fact of the matter was that Mr. and Mrs. Brew were in many ways rather different from Mr. and Mrs. Godden, and lots of the other fishermen said they couldn't think how Ben Godden could get along with such an unsatisfactory partner. Arthur Brew sometimes drank too much, and then he would have a headache next day, and shout at his wife, and hit Tony and Betty if they were silly enough to stay within reach. And then, of course, he would slack at his work when the boat went out that night, because he was feeling ill with all the drink he had taken, and so Ben would have to do most of the work. He was not like that all the time, of course, but it did happen sometimes, and Mrs. Godden used to get very cross about it.

"Why don't you get another partner, Ben?" she would cry indignantly.

"And what would happen to poor old Arthur then, eh?" Ben would ask with a smile. "He'd only go from bad to worse, poor chap. I'm hoping he'll pull himself together one of these days, and if I can help him to do it, I will."

"Well, I'm sure no one else would have the patience," Mrs. Godden would say. "I'm sure I wouldn't."

Then her husband would laugh and give her a kiss, and the argument would be over.

That was another thing Jack noticed about the difference between his family and the people in the next-door cottage; the Brews often had rows and his parents never did. He could not remember a really angry word; even when he had been naughty, and of course that happened sometimes, his mother and father seemed more sorry than angry; and although he did have to be punished sometimes too, there was never anything unkind about it. He saw the point of it, and when it was all over they were as good friends as ever, while

Mrs. Brew would go on grumbling about a thing for days and days.

The biggest difference of all, perhaps, was on Sundays. On Sunday morning Mum cooked the dinner—and a jolly fine dinner it was, too—while Jack was dressed up in his best clothes and sent off to morning Sunday School. Dad also put on his best clothes and took Baby for a walk in her pram, and as soon as Sunday School was over he would be outside the hall waiting for Jack, and the two of them—no, the three of them, if you counted Nellie—went for a walk. Morning Sunday School was usually very short, and Ben Godden would ask his son all about it, and woe betide Jack if he could not give interesting answers! His father knew a lot about the Bible, because he read a bit in it every evening, sometimes aloud and sometimes quietly to himself, so if Jack got the lessons mixed up through not attending, his father knew all about it, and soon put him right.

Of course their walk always ended up on the bit of beach where the boats were, because they both loved the sea and loved boats so much. They might start off by the side of the canal, or through the town, or even up the hill towards Lympne aerodrome, but sooner or later their footsteps would turn back towards the sea and the *Mary Uden*.

They would talk, and potter about the boat, and Baby would go to sleep in the sunshine, and then suddenly Dad would look at the big silver watch that had belonged to his grandfather and which he always carried in his pocket, and exclaim that it was late and they would get into trouble if they did not hurry.

"Mum will be waiting for us with the rolling pin!" he'd say with a grin, and Jack would laugh because he knew that was the last thing his mother would ever do.

After dinner it was Sunday School again for Jack, while Dad helped Mum with the washing-up before they settled down for a Sunday-afternoon nap. There was always a cake for tea on Sundays, and sometimes Jack brought Tony and Betty in to tea, if he had been able to persuade them to go to Sunday School with him.

On Sunday evening Mum put on her best hat, and dressed Baby Nellie up in her best dress, and they all went to church. Baby did not go inside, of course—as Jack said she would only have made a row and put everybody off. She went to sleep in her pram in the porch or outside in the sunshine, according to the weather. They all sat rather near the door in case she took it into her head to cry, but she seldom did.

Well, that was the difference between the Goddens and the Brews, for the Brews never went to church at all, and got out of Sunday School if they could. Mrs. Brew did not care whether Tony and Betty went or not, and sometimes dinner was not over in time for them to get ready and go. Jack always called for them hopefully, and if they were ready and felt inclined to go, he was delighted. Sometimes they tried to persuade him not to go, and told him of

wonderful plans they had made for that afternoon, but although he sometimes wished he could
join them when there was something really good
planned, yet he knew how surprised and sorry
his father and mother would be if he played
truant, and how disappointed his Sunday School
teacher, Mr. Emsworth—the curate—would be
if he did not turn up in his usual place.

He thoroughly enjoyed Sunday School as a
rule, and it was only when Tony and Betty tried
to tempt him with something very exciting that
he wished for a moment that he need not go.
But he always did go, and before the end of the
afternoon he had quite forgotten that he had
wanted to do something else, and was perfectly
happy where he was.

He was very fond of the curate, Mr. Emsworth,
who managed to make his lessons very interesting.
He made lots of jokes, too, and was a very jolly
sort of person. The children did not like it quite
as well on the rare occasions when the vicar,
Mr. Barton, came to take them, because although
he was very kind he used very long words, and
they did not always know what he was talking
about. He never made jokes, either. But Jack's
father and mother liked him, and said he was
very nice.

Well, that is what the Godden family were
like, and the Brew family, and now we must go
back to the cottage where Jack is eating his
bread and dripping, and Mrs. Godden is looking
restlessly out of the window, wondering what has
delayed her husband.

Suddenly she caught the sound of footsteps and sprang to her feet, relief showing on her face.

"Here he comes!" she exclaimed.

"Gosh, you've got quick ears, Mum," said Jack, "I didn't hear anything."

"I'd know your dad's footsteps anywhere," said Mrs. Godden, hurrying to the stove to make a fresh pot of tea. Then she ran to the gate just as the footsteps reached it, and caught her husband by the arm.

"I thought you were never coming," she said.

Ben Godden bent and kissed her.

"I'm all right," he said. "You shouldn't worry about me."

Behind him a tall, sulky-looking man nodded to Mrs. Godden before going in at the next gate. Nobody was waiting there for him.

"All my fault," he said. "I had a rotten bad head. Ben will tell you all about it, I daresay."

"Ben doesn't grumble, if that's what you mean," said Mrs. Godden sharply.

"Where's my cup of tea?" asked Ben, leading his angry little wife firmly towards the cottage door. "So long, Arthur; see you to-night."

"Hullo, Dad," said Jack as his father came in. "I'm glad you've come, 'cause I'm just going to school."

"Wipe the crumbs off your face, lad," said his father with a grin.

"Did anything happen?" asked Jack, doing as he was told.

"Nothing at all. What should happen?"

"Well, you might have got drownded, you was so late," said Jack.

"I'm here, aren't I? Now you cut along off to school, son, and don't get ideas into your head. So long."

Jack said good-bye to his father, his mother and Baby, and went off to school, while Ben took the cup of tea that his wife handed to him, and answered her questioning gaze with a nod.

"Yes, he was queer," he said. "But I don't want to talk about it. We're safe home—the Lord be thanked. But . . . poor chap, I'm sorry for him."

Chapter 2

JACK AT SCHOOL

IF anyone asked Jack if he liked school, he grinned and said that he liked holidays a good deal better. Really, he was quite happy at school, did fairly well, was neither at the top nor the bottom of the class, and did not get into trouble more than most people.

Tony Brew sat beside him in class, and sometimes Miss Lee, the teacher, got exasperated when they were troublesome and separated them. That always made them very gloomy, and they would really try to behave for a bit after that.

On this particular morning, after Jack's father had come back late from his night's fishing, Jack was trotting along the road as usual when he heard running feet behind him, and turned to see Tony and Betty racing after him.

"Hullo," he said as they came up. "Your dad looked in a bit of a wax this morning, didn't he?"

"He was," said Tony gruffly. "He wouldn't let me eat my bread and jam—said I'd be late—and I'd only just started it."

"Well, you would have been late if you'd waited much longer," said Jack.

"Yes, but I'm hungry," objected Tony.

"It's your own fault; you ought to get up when Mum calls you," said Betty crossly.

"Mum was late too," Tony pointed out.

"Yes, but you didn't get up when she called you; you pretended to be asleep, and she had to come right upstairs for you," said Betty.

"And then she clouted me," said Tony. "It didn't hurt, though. And when I did get up I couldn't finish my breakfast. It isn't fair."

"Do you always get up when your mother calls?" Jack asked Betty. She was looking so prim and smug as she told Tony where he had gone wrong that Jack wanted to know if she was always good.

"Of course I do," said Betty.

"Ooh, you don't!" cried Tony angrily. "You know you don't. You were late for school twice last week."

"That's a fib," shouted Betty. "It was only once."

"Twice! Twice! Twice!" chanted Tony, dodging out of the way as his sister tried to hit him.

"Oh, shut up, you two," said Jack crossly. "You'll get a glass of milk at break, Tony, and I'll give you half my slice of cake. Now do be quiet and come in to school."

The children were already lining up in the playground, ready to march in to school, and the senior boy was standing with the late book in his hand by the gate, to write down the names of latecomers, as the three ran in. Jack and Tony darted into the line among their friends, and Betty went in more leisurely style along to where her own cronies were standing. Then the bell rang and they all marched in.

A good many of the children had fathers who

were fishermen, and it was surprising how the
story of the *Mary Uden* coming in late had got
round the school. Some fathers had come home
saying that they wouldn't be surprised if Ben
Godden broke his partnership with a man who
could let him down so badly, and some of the
children were unkind enough to ask Jack and
Tony during break if that was so.

Tony turned very red and looked miserable,
and Jack rushed to the rescue.

"What a silly thing to say!" he scoffed. "Do
you think my dad would break partnership with
Mr. Brew because he'd had a headache? I heard
him say to my mum that he'd got a rotten head,
and you don't think my dad would be hard on
him for that, do you?"

"Ah, yes, but how did he get his rotten head?"
asked one of the older boys with a snigger, and
Tony looked as if he could burst into tears.

"I expect he knocked it," said Jack valiantly.
"Come on, Tony—I've made a new glider. Let's
try it out."

So they tried out the new glider, which Jack
had made out of a page from the back of his
exercise book, and ate their cake and drank
their bottle of milk. Then the bell rang for school
again, and they all rushed in.

So far Jack had managed not to get into
trouble at all that morning, but such a fine state
of affairs could not possibly last. He found Miss
Lee, with a face like a thunder-cloud, waiting by
his desk when he got into the classroom. In her
hand was his exercise book.

"Jack, have you been tearing pages out of this book?" she demanded.

"Say no," whispered Tony, but although Jack was rather scared, he thought he had better own up. He knew what his father thought about people who told fibs, and he would rather endure any punishment than disappoint Dad.

"Yes, miss," he said.

"Then you'll have to go to the headmaster," she said angrily. She shut the book with a clap and handed it to him. "Show him this and tell him why I sent you. Go along—now."

Jack took the book and went out of the room. He did not in the least want to go to the headmaster; he knew that visits of this sort usually meant the cane. He went slowly down the corridor towards the Head's study, and then went on past it, thinking he could pretend to be going to the cloakroom for a handkerchief. He waited in the cloakroom for a minute or two, and then started off again. What would happen if he went back to Miss Lee and said he had seen the headmaster? Or just said that he couldn't find him? But it would be telling fibs again, and he didn't want to do that if he could help it. He had done it occasionally, and always felt terribly mean afterwards. Dad had talked to him about it, and he had promised not to do it again. So he walked more and more slowly past the headmaster's room again, and wished that something would happen—a fire or an accident or something—so that everyone would have something else to think about and he wouldn't be caned.

He went past, but he turned back again. Then suddenly the door opened. Mr. Harris, the headmaster, had heard those slow, hesitating footsteps, and knew quite well what they meant. Now he looked out and saw Jack.

"Do you want to see me, Jack?" he asked.

Jack gulped. " Yes, sir," he said.

"Come in. Now," said Mr. Harris, closing the door, "what's it all about?"

Jack held out the exercise book, open at the place where the pages had been torn out.

"Miss Lee said I was to show you this," he said.

"Oh, yes." Mr. Harris examined the book. "Did you tear the pages out?"

"Yes, sir."

"How did Miss Lee find out?"

"I suppose she looked in the book, sir."

"But how did she know you had done it yourself?"

"She asked me, sir."

"And you owned up?"

"Yes, sir," said Jack, feeling very glad he had not told a fib to Miss Lee.

"And why did you destroy your exercise book?" was the next question.

"I—I wanted to make a glider, sir."

"And you made one?"

"Yes, sir."

"Did it fly?" asked Mr. Harris.

Jack brightened up.

"Rather, it did! It was wizard, sir. It flew right across the playground—well, nearly—well, more than half-way, sir."

"I see. But, you know, your exercise book is given to you for work, not for making gliders. It isn't really given to you at all, it's just for your school use—do you see what I mean?"

"Yes, sir," sighed Jack.

"You knew that really, didn't you?"

"I suppose so, sir."

"You knew that you couldn't take it home and draw in it, for instance?"

"Oh, yes, sir."

"So if you had stopped to think, you would have known you were doing wrong?"

"Yes, sir, I suppose so," said Jack, thinking that this was where the cane came in.

However, Mr. Harris did not go to the famous cupboard where the cane was kept. Instead he handed the book back to Jack.

"I want your word of honour that you won't tear up books that don't belong to you again. Get any paper you want for gliders out of the waste-paper basket. And if there isn't any there, come and ask me."

"Thank you, sir," said Jack with a sigh of relief.

"Word of honour?" asked the headmaster.

"Word of honour, sir, I won't ever tear up books again," said Jack.

"Right. Now go back to your classroom. Shut the door quietly—that's right."

Miss Lee looked at Jack suspiciously as he went in.

"What did the headmaster say?" she asked sharply.

"He said I must get paper for gliders out of the waste-paper basket, miss," said Jack.

Miss Lee compressed her lips. In her opinion the headmaster was not nearly stern enough with the boys—or with the girls either.

"Go back to your desk," she said. "And if I catch you tearing your books again——" She left the threat unuttered, and hoped that Jack would be suitably terrified.

Jack, however, settled down to try and catch up with the rest of the class in the arithmetic lesson, of which he had missed nearly half. They were doing a new kind of sum, and he had to ask Tony how to do it. Tony was not very sure himself, and so Miss Lee had the satisfaction of marking Jack's book with a big cross in red ink when she came to it, although she knew quite well that he had missed the explanations at the beginning of the lesson, and could not really be expected to know how to do the sums by himself.

That evening at tea Jack told his mother and father about the day's doings at school, and when he came to the part about the sums his father told him to write down the question, and he would try and show him how to do it. But they made an awful muddle of it between them, for Ben Godden was not very good at sums, and things were done differently nowadays from the way they were done when he was a boy at school. So they were all looking very hot and bothered, leaning over the kitchen table, when they heard a cooee from the garden, and Tony and Betty shouted to Jack to come out and play.

"Hi, Betty!" called Mr. Godden. "Come and see if you can show Jack how to do this sum. I'm blest if I can remember how they go."

Betty came in, full of importance.

"Oh yes, I'll show him, Mr. Godden," she said. "We did them last year. They're easy as easy!" She settled herself down on a chair at the table and proceeded to make everything clear to Jack and his father.

"I see," said Ben Godden, watching intently. "Yes, of course that's it. Set out another, Betty, and I'll have a go."

So Jack's father did a sum, and then Jack did a couple, and then the three children went out to play.

"She's a bright little monkey," said Ben to his wife when they had gone.

"Funny-tempered, like the rest of the family," said Mrs. Godden.

"Well, they've no reason to be anything else, poor souls. It's a funny sort of life to live, with no place for God in it anywhere. But it'll all come right some day—you'll see."

"You want a miracle, you do!" laughed his wife.

"And why not? The Lord hasn't forgotten how to work miracles, I suppose! It's a fresh miracle every time a man or woman, boy or girl, turns sincerely to God, and it's happening every day. I've not given up hopes of the Brews, not by a long way. I shan't be a bit surprised when they're converted—all the lot of 'em."

"Well, I shall," said Mrs. Godden.

Chapter 3

TWO YOUNG SCAMPS

"I'VE got an idea," said Jack.

Tony brightened up. It was always Jack who had the ideas, and mostly, from the boys' point of view, they were good ones. From the point of view of parents, teachers, and other grown-ups they were not always quite so good, but perhaps that was not entirely to be expected.

"What is it?" asked Tony expectantly.

"Have you ever been a stowaway?" asked Jack, dropping his voice to a whisper, although they were alone on the beach and no one could possibly have heard him if he had spoken at the top of his voice.

Tony's eyes grew round with excitement.

"On a liner or something, do you mean? A voyage to Australia or France?"

"Something like that," said Jack grandly. "But I think we ought to put in a bit of practice first, don't you? Just to see if we can do it. I vote we stow away on the *Mary Uden* to-night, shall we?"

Tony jumped with delight.

"Gosh, what an idea! But what will your dad say when he finds us?"

"Well," said Jack, who had thought everything out, "if your dad's got a headache he'll be jolly glad of our help—I should think," he added doubtfully.

"My dad never has a headache two nights running," said Tony offendedly.

"Well, anyway, that doesn't matter," said Jack, who did not want to think too much about the awkward side of the business. Tony had no wish to dwell on that side of it either, in case Jack changed his mind and said he would not go. Both young scamps thought it would be a fine thing to stow away on the boat, and, as usual when people want to do anything very badly, they both shut their eyes to the matter of whether they ought to do it or not.

"Here comes Betty—shall we tell her?" asked Tony, as he caught sight of his sister running across the beach towards them.

"She'll find out, anyway; she always does," said Jack.

"She'll want to come too," said Tony warningly.

"She couldn't. There's no such thing as a girl stowaway. And besides, she'll be useful if Mum gets in a stew about it, and wonders where we are." Jack raised his voice in a shout. "Hi! Betty! Come here a minute. I want to tell you something."

Betty was coming towards them as fast as she could, and was quite out of breath by the time she reached them.

"What is it?" she panted.

"First of all you've got to promise you won't split on us," said Jack.

"Promise. What is it?" asked Betty.

"We're going to stow away on the *Mary Uden* to-night," said Jack in an impressive whisper.

"Me too," said Betty promptly.

"You can't. For one thing there isn't room, and for another there's no such thing as a girl stowaway," said Jack.

"Well, I could be the first," said Betty discontentedly, kicking the pebbles with her sandal.

"Of course you can't. There isn't any such thing, I tell you. And besides, you've got to be there to tell Mum where we are if she gets upset. Wait till we've gone, of course, when she can't do anything about it, and don't say anything unless she's in a real stew, and talking about going to the police, or something."

Betty argued for a little longer, but without much hope. In her heart she agreed with Jack's ruling; she had never heard of a girl stowaway and so she was really ready to accept that it was an adventure for boys only. She argued for a little while, just to show them that they could not have all their own way too easily, but in the end she gave in and promised to do what they asked.

"But why don't you go to bed as usual and then climb out of the window?" she asked.

"Because they're catching an early tide to-night, before my bedtime," said Jack promptly.

"Well, why don't you put it off till they're going out on a late tide, then?" asked Betty. "It would be much easier."

But neither of the boys would hear of putting

off their great adventure now that they had set their minds on it, and in fact both felt that they ought to be making their arrangements already. It would be fatal if either of their fathers came down to get the boat ready before they had safely hidden themselves.

So Betty went home and the two boys scouted carefully over to where the *Mary Uden* was lying. They clambered aboard, after first taking a good look round to see if anyone was watching them, and bobbed their heads down below the sides as soon as they could.

"Where shall we hide?" asked Tony, his voice shaking with excitement.

"At the back of the sail locker. Dad's got some old sails that he never uses right at the back, and if we get behind them they'll never see us."

So they got into the sail locker and burrowed their way to the back, making regular little nests for themselves among the heavy canvas.

"It's jolly hot in here," muttered Tony after a while.

"We can leave the door open till they come," said Jack, preparing to feel his way forward in the darkness, but at that moment footsteps and voices sounded near at hand, and they knew that they had lost their opportunity.

Nothing else happened for a while; the two men were getting their nets ready in leisurely style, exchanging a few cheery words with other fishermen engaged in the same tasks on either side of them. Then at last came the unmistakable scrunch as the boat was hauled down to the sea, and in a few moments the rough jolting gave place to a smooth rise and fall that told them they were on the water.

"We're off!" murmured Tony in an excited whisper.

"Hush," said Jack automatically.

Tony was silent. They could hear footsteps on the deck, and the murmur of voices. The boat heeled over a little, and they knew that a fresh breeze was catching the sails. On and on they went, rising and falling gently, and in the end the two boys fell asleep.

Jack did not know how long they slept, but he awoke to hear Tony whimpering beside him.

"What's the matter?" he asked fiercely.

"It's too hot in here. I want to go home," said Tony.

"Don't be silly—you can't go home. Lie still."

"I can't. It's too hot. I shall be sick," said poor Tony.

"Open the door, then," said Jack. "Perhaps they won't notice if they're busy."

Tony started to feel his way towards the place where he supposed the door to be, but began to whimper again after a moment or two.

"I can't find it," he whined.

"You'll give the whole show away in a minute," said Jack. "Look out—I'll come."

Meanwhile the two men were busy on deck, and had no idea of what was going on below. But suddenly Mr. Brew turned to his partner with a puzzled look.

"I believe there's a cat in the sail locker," he said.

"A cat? Why?" asked Mr. Godden.

"There's something in there. Listen." was the reply.

"So there is," exclaimed Ben Godden. "Bumping around like anything. I'll let it out, but take care it doesn't jump overboard in its fright when I open the door."

He opened the door, but great was his surprise when he saw in front of him not a cat but his own son and Tony.

"Jack!" he cried in astonishment.

"Yes, Dad. I'm a stowaway," said the boy, half proud and half frightened.

"Is that Tony?" cried Mr. Brew. "Why, you little varmint—what are you doing there? I'll tan the hide off you when I get you home, for this!"

"What's the idea, Jack?" asked Ben Godden gravely. "Does your mum know? But of course she doesn't—she wouldn't let you do this."

"We told Betty to tell Mum if she got frightened," said Jack. "We—we wanted to be stowaways. Only it got so hot in there that we wanted to get out."

"And what would have happened if you hadn't attracted our attention?" asked Mr. Godden. "Supposing I'd locked the sail locker, as I sometimes do, when we got ashore again? You'd both have been dead before we found you. That's a nice thing to happen, isn't it?"

"I never thought of that," said Jack, crestfallen at his father's words.

"I don't suppose you did. But you did know that it's my rule that you don't come to sea in term time, now didn't you?"

"Yes, Dad," said Jack.

"Well, now they're here, they can do a spot of work," said Mr. Brew impatiently. "They've been to sea before and they know the ropes. Get a move on, you lads, and haul the net up."

For the next hour the boys were kept very busy, and thoroughly enjoyed it all. The sight of the gleaming fish tumbling about in the net fascinated them, and tossing the catch into the hold made them feel like old hands at the job. Those that were too small to sell were thrown back into the sea again or cut up for bait, and the two men saw to it that their stowaways were kept very busy.

"What about some cocoa, Dad?" asked Jack when a burst of activity was over for the time being, and they were sailing to a fresh ground.

"Right—you go below to the galley and make some," said his father, and Jack hurried down to the tiny stove, taking the ship's lantern with him. It was bright moonlight up on deck, and the mast-head lights were gleaming brightly, but down below in the galley it was rather dark, and as he hung the lantern on its hook it swung slowly to and fro, making weird shadows move in the corners.

However, Jack was not the sort of boy to be afraid of shadows, and he lit the stove and got about the business of making the cocoa confidently. He found an opened tin of condensed milk, and put generous spoonfuls into each cup. Then he put in the cocoa and mixed it up together into a paste. Then the kettle boiled and he poured on the water, and the hot drink was ready.

"I wish I could do this every night," he said, when he reached the deck again. "It's such fun."

"You can when you're a man," said his father. "But till then you've got to do as you're told, and go to school, and learn all they can teach you. A fine fisherman you'd be if you couldn't read or write, or do sums enough to sell your fish."

"I can read," said Jack indignantly. "And my writing isn't as bad as it was last year. And I'm getting on well in arithmetic."

"Well, they teach you other things too," said his father. "I wish they taught you to be obedient."

Jack crimsoned at this rebuke, and said nothing.

"We'll have a talk about that later on," said his father. "I think you boys had better shake down on that coil of rope now and get some sleep, or you'll be fit for nothing to-morrow."

So they lay down on the coil of rope, and Mr. Godden threw an old sail over them to keep them warm, and they were soon fast asleep again.

Chapter 4

TWO WORRIED MOTHERS

SHORTLY after the *Mary Uden* left Hythe, Mrs. Godden began to wonder where Jack was. It was past his bedtime, and she did not like him to be too late. Baby Nellie was fast asleep, and the cottage was very quiet. Where could Jack be?

She went to look in the little garden, but he was not there. Then she went to the front gate and stared up and down the road, but he was not playing cricket with a group of boys a little farther down, nor was he with some other boys who were racing about on roller skates. No, she could not see him anywhere.

At the end of the road farthest away from the sea was the recreation ground, a big open space covered with grass, separated by a road from the canal. Mrs. Godden thought her son would probably be there, and ran down the road to find him. She was beginning to feel rather cross with him; he knew perfectly well what time he should come in to go to bed, and she half thought of letting him go without his supper, for being so naughty.

However, he was not on the recreation ground, and she wondered where on earth she should look next. She went home again, and even peeped into his bedroom in case he had come in and gone to bed while she was out looking for him, but he was not there.

She looked at Baby to make sure she was all right, and then went round and tapped on the door of Mrs. Brew's cottage. Mrs. Brew opened the door, and Mrs. Godden could see Betty sitting at the table, eating some corn-flakes, but Tony was not there.

"Is Tony in?" asked Mrs. Godden quickly.

"No, he isn't, and I'm going to tan him when he does come in," said Mrs. Brew angrily. "He's no business to stop out so late, and he knows it."

"They must be together, then," said Mrs. Godden. "Jack isn't in either. I wonder where they can have got to?"

Betty went on quietly eating her supper, and did not say a word. Neither of the women thought of asking her, and she kept very quiet so that they would not notice her.

"They're always getting into mischief, those two," said Mrs. Brew. "I'm sure Tony wouldn't think of half the naughty things he does unless Jack led him into trouble."

"Boys are all the same," said Mrs. Godden. "Always doing things they shouldn't. But I wish I knew where they were, all the same."

"He shan't have a bite of supper when he comes in," said Mrs. Brew.

"I don't think Jack will, either," said Mrs. Godden. She turned to go. "Let me know if Tony turns up, will you?"

"I will," said Mrs. Brew, and Mrs. Godden went home again.

Betty had finished her corn-flakes, and now slipped very quietly up to bed. Usually she begged for another ten minutes, and argued until her mother was cross with her, but to-night she was very good and quiet, and was in bed and pretending to be asleep when her mother came upstairs.

Mrs. Brew now began to do what Mrs. Godden had done a short time previously. She searched the garden and looked in the tool-shed, and then went to the front and stared up and down the road. There were only a few big boys out now, as the younger ones had been called in by their mothers, and she shouted to one of them.

"Sid! Have you seen Tony and Jack anywhere?"

"No, Mrs. Brew," was the reply. "I haven't seen them since tea-time."

"Well, if you do see them, send them home at once, will you?" she said, and the boy promised to do so.

Both mothers were now getting seriously worried. Of course both Jack and Tony knew their way about Hythe quite well, and were not likely to be lost, but supposing they had taken a mad freak and got on a bus for Folkestone or Dymchurch? Or supposing they had fallen in the canal and were drowned? This last thought occurred to Mrs. Godden with such force that she went and tapped on Mrs. Brew's door again.

"I can't rest," she said, "while those boys are missing. Will you listen for Baby while I go out and look for them?"

Mrs. Brew agreed to do this, and Mrs. Godden set off. Betty, upstairs in bed, heard what was said and wondered if she ought to tell her mother where they were. But she was rather frightened, and knew that she would get into trouble for not telling what she knew earlier. So she shut her eyes and snuggled down under the blankets, and pretended to be asleep again.

While Mrs. Godden was hurrying down towards the canal she met Mr. Emsworth, the curate. He was struck by her worried look, and stopped her.

"Anything the matter, Mrs. Godden?"

"It's Jack and Tony, sir," she answered. "They haven't come home and I don't know where they are."

Mr. Emsworth whistled.

"Have you any idea where they were going?"

"None at all. They usually go out to play together after tea till bedtime, and they often are a bit late, but never as late as this. They know quite well that it's long past their bedtime, and I'm so afraid they may have come to some harm."

Mr. Emsworth thought for a moment or two.

"I'll get some of the senior Scouts to come and hunt for them," he said. "The little blighters! Now don't you worry, Mrs. Godden. I don't for one minute believe that they've come to any harm. They're a couple of high-spirited young scamps, but they've gone a bit too far this time. We'll do our best to find them."

So Mrs. Godden went home again, and told

Mrs. Brew what the curate was going to do. And Betty, upstairs in bed, heard too and quaked with fear. She would surely get into terrible trouble if she told what she knew now, so she shut her eyes tighter than ever and snuggled down more deeply under the bedclothes.

Meanwhile Mr. Emsworth called on half-a-dozen of his senior Scouts, and told them what had happened.

"We'll quarter the town and have a thorough search," he said. "Someone may have given them the money to go to the cinema, and they may be scared to come home so late. We must check up on all the cinemas, or any other place where they might be amusing themselves. You, Terry, patrol the beach; Lawrence and Guy, you go right along the canal—they might have thought of going fishing there; the rest of us will divide up the town."

So the Scouts cheerfully put aside whatever it was they were doing, and set off on their quest. They searched the town, they searched the beach, and they searched the canal area, but of course they did not find the boys. Mr. Emsworth, very tired after cycling up and down the steep hills behind the town, made a last call on the cottage in Sandgate Lane. He could see by the light burning in the kitchen window that Mrs. Godden was still up and waiting, and he tapped and went in.

"No good news, I'm afraid," he said, meeting her anxious glance. "I'm sure you ought to call in the police."

"I didn't want to do that," said Mrs. Godden. "If they find the boys will they take them away?"

"Of course not," said the curate. "They may give them a good fright if they find they've just been playing a trick on you, but they'll be very kind, and they can do things that we can't. I mean, they'll telephone descriptions of them to all the other police stations in the country, and sooner or later they'll be bound to be identified and picked up. I really advise you to see them, Mrs. Godden. I'll come with you, if you like."

"It's very kind of you," said Mrs. Godden, feeling relieved. "I'll just see poor Mrs. Brew; she must be as worried as I am."

So Mrs. Godden and Mr. Emsworth went in to the next-door cottage, where Mrs. Brew was sitting in front of the fire crying. Betty had been to sleep, but she was very uneasy, and woke up at the slightest sound. Now she heard Mr. Emsworth's voice, and crept to the top of the stairs to hear what he was saying.

The curate was repeating the arguments in favour of calling in the police, and Betty's knees knocked together as she heard them decide to follow his advice. Now she had got to confess! She had promised the boys to tell their mothers if it got as far as that. She put on a coat over her nightdress and crept slowly down the stairs.

"Are you going to the police about the boys?" she asked nervously.

They turned in surprise at the sound of her voice.

"Now you run along back to bed like a good girl," said her mother.

"Well, please don't go to the police," said Betty pleadingly.

"You don't understand. You want your brother to be found, don't you?" asked Mr. Emsworth rather severely.

"He might be kidnapped," said Mrs. Brew with a sob.

"He isn't. He's a stowaway," said Betty, trembling.

"A what?" cried Mrs. Godden.

"Here! What do you know about all this?" asked Mr. Emsworth. He sat down and drew the little girl towards him. "You know where they are, do you?"

Betty nodded silently.

"Tell me, then. Stowaways? Where?"

"In the *Mary Uden.*"

"That's our boat!" cried Mrs. Godden in amazement.

"Yes," whimpered Betty.

"Oh, you naughty girl—you knew all the time!" cried Mrs. Brew angrily.

Betty began to cry, and Mrs. Godden felt as though she really could smack her.

"How do you know that's what they've done?" asked Mr. Emsworth quietly.

"They told me," sobbed Betty. "And they made me promise not to tell unless Mum was going to the police."

"Well, you shouldn't have given such a promise, really," said the curate. "You see what a lot of trouble it's given everybody. We should all be in bed and asleep now—Scouts and all—if you'd told your mother in the beginning where they were."

"I couldn't sneak, and I had promised," said Betty.

"Yes," said the curate thoughtfully. "It's the boys' fault. Well, you run along back to bed, and I'll get in touch with the Scouts and call them off. Good-night, Mrs. Brew. Good-night, Mrs. Godden. Don't be too hard on them when they come home."

He went out, and the two women looked at each other.

"To think of them doing that!" exclaimed Mrs. Brew.

"I don't know what they'll think of next, I'm sure," said Mrs. Godden wearily. "Well, I'm going to bed. Oh, dear! We never thanked Mr. Emsworth for all he'd done."

"I wonder what you asked him to help for?" asked Mrs. Brew. "I'm sure I'd never think of asking a curate."

"He's ever so good," said Mrs. Godden, "and he knows the boys and they know him. They're in his Sunday School class, you know."

"I never thought churchy people were much good," said Mrs. Brew. "Stuck-up, most of them are."

"You can't call Mr. Emsworth stuck-up," said Mrs. Godden. "And I've always found church people just the ones to help if you're in trouble. I'm sure no one could have done more than he did to-night—and the Scouts too, of course. Well, good-night, Mrs. Brew. I don't suppose it'll be long before they're in, now. It was an early tide to-night."

"Good-night," said Mrs. Brew.

Chapter 5

IN DISGRACE

THE moon was setting by the time the *Mary Uden* came in on a high tide and was drawn up on the beach by the two men. The hold where the catch was lying was covered with a tarpaulin for the time being, and the two fathers lifted their sleeping sons and carried them home.

Jack did not wake up even when his father undid his shoes and took them off, and rolled him up in his bedclothes. Then Ben Godden went into his own room, where his wife roused up enough to ask anxiously if he had found the boy.

"Yes, I found him, the little monkey," said Ben grimly. "I'll have a talk with him in the morning. Were you scared?"

"I was a bit," admitted Mrs. Godden. "I couldn't think what had become of him, and Mr. Emsworth helped me, and so did the Scouts. Half the people in Hythe knew they were missing, and it wasn't until we were on the point of going for the police that Betty—little monkey that she is—told us where they were."

"Kids are thoughtless," said Ben Godden. "Oh, well, let's hope it'll be a lesson to him."

Next day Jack could not believe it was morning when his mother called him to get up. He blinked and blinked, but the sun was shining and he could hear things going on out in the lane, and he had to believe that it was breakfast-time.

He came downstairs yawning, and turned very red when he saw his father at the table.

"Come in, son," said Mr. Godden gravely. "Now I want you to hear how unhappy you made your mother last night. She lost half her night's sleep hunting for you, and so did the curate and the Scouts."

"Golly!" cried Jack in horror. "Were they all looking for us? Why didn't Betty stop them?"

"Betty said she'd promised you not to say anything unless we were going to the police," said Mrs. Godden.

"Well, I meant her to tell you if you got worried, Mum," mumbled Jack, feeling very much ashamed of himself. "I didn't mean you to worry, honestly."

"It wasn't only me," said Mrs. Godden. "What Mr. Emsworth thought about it all I can't think. Nor the Scouts."

"Now listen to me, my lad," said Ben, thinking the boy had had enough. "I'll just say this: you thought it would be a bit of an adventure, but it was flat disobedience. You knew we didn't allow you out in the boat all night in term time. And it was unkind thoughtlessness—you made your mother, and lots of other people too, very worried and very tired. So it don't look so good, seen that way, does it?"

Jack gulped and nodded. Tears were gathering in his eyes, and he began to see how his nice little adventure had appeared to other people.

"I'm ever so sorry, Mum," he said.

His father got up, smiled, and patted him on the shoulder.

"Well, don't do it again, and we'll say no more about it. And next time you think up a fine, adventurous idea, think how it's going to affect other people, see? Now sit down and have your breakfast."

Jack brushed the tears away with the back of his hand, and sat down to his porridge. He did feel terribly sleepy after his exciting night, and he wished he could go back to bed instead of having to go to school. He did not like to ask, however, and so he finished his porridge, said he did not want any bread and jam, and set off with rather dawdling steps down the lane.

"Poor little lad—he ought to go back to bed," said his mother compassionately.

"You let him go to school," said his father. "He's got to learn that if you have your fun you must pay for it. We haven't punished him, but he'll have to find out that nature itself will punish him when he does wrong. What a kid doesn't realize is that if you disobey its laws and rules, it comes back on you somehow, every time. Now he'll feel tired and off-colour all day, and he's sharp enough to know it's because he was awake half the night. Well, other times when he did it with permission, we let him lie in all the morning afterwards, so he didn't feel tired. But this time he did it off his own bat, against our wishes, and he must take the consequences."

As Jack slouched wearily down the lane he

heard Tony and Betty behind him. They were not running light-heartedly as they did on other days, but dragging along much as he was doing himself, and he turned and waited for them.

He was sorry in a minute or two that he had done so, for they both glowered at him sullenly.

"Nice sort of ideas you have," grumbled Betty. "I won't play with you any more, Jack Godden."

" Did you get into a row?" asked Jack.

"Dad tanned us," said Tony. He wriggled. "I shan't be able to sit down for days."

"What did he do that for? It was my idea," said Jack.

"Didn't your father tan you?" asked Betty.

"No," said Jack. "I promised I wouldn't do it again, though."

"Why did you promise, if he didn't tan you?" asked Tony.

"Well, it was the way he talked," said Jack, feeling rather foolish. "I did give a lot of trouble to a lot of people, and when he sort of pointed that out I could see it. So I said I wouldn't do it again."

"You'll forget," said Betty with a loud laugh.

"No, I shan't," declared Jack. "I—I really am sorry I upset Mum."

"I'm not," said Tony vengefully. "I'd like to run right away and get lost so's they never find me, and then they'd stop up all night looking for me and I'd laugh!"

"You wouldn't laugh because you wouldn't know," said Betty scornfully. "And they'd set the

police on you and catch you, easy as anything.
Mr. Emsworth was telling us about that last
night. He says the police can find anyone easy
as winking. They telephone all the other police
stations and they all keep a look-out, and where-
ever you get to, they soon find you."

"Why don't they find all the thieves and
murderers, then?" asked Tony. "If it's as easy
as all that, I mean."

"They do, mostly," said Jack. "My dad says
it's only when a man's too big a fool to earn an
honest living that he turns crook, and the police
always get him in the end."

That seemed to end the conversation, but when
they got to school they found that the fame of
their exploits had preceded them. Some of the
Scouts who had taken part in the hunt on the
previous evening were not too pleased about the
way it had turned out, and came up to ask a few
questions. Jack and Tony and Betty were quite
glad when the bell rang for them to go in to
school.

Chapter 6

MISS LEE IS DISGUSTED

POOR Jack—his luck was quite out that morning. He was glad to get into the classroom, away from the big boys in the playground who wanted to make it clear to him that they did not think his behaviour particularly funny. But no sooner were prayers over and lessons begun that he began to feel outrageously sleepy again.

Miss Lee stopped short on seeing a tremendous yawn, and attacked him at once.

"Well, Jack, I'm sorry you find my lessons so boring," she said acidly. "Perhaps you'd better tell the headmaster that you can't keep awake while I'm talking to you, and see what he thinks about it."

Jack kept silence, but his face went red. She stared at him for a moment and then went on teaching. But Jack knew that she was watching him, and when he felt another yawn rising in his throat, he tried to keep it back, and tears rose in his eyes with the effort.

"Dear me, I didn't know there was anything to make you cry in a simple geography lesson, Jack Godden," said Miss Lee sarcastically. "Tell me what I've said to upset you?"

"Nothing, miss," mumbled Jack, and luckily for him Tony was now caught in a tremendous yawn.

"I'd like to know what's the matter with all you children?" cried Miss Lee angrily. "Tony, you're doing it on purpose. Stop it at once."

The other children now began to think that it was all a joke, and yawns broke out on every side. Miss Lee was very angry indeed, and it was not until she threatened to send the whole form to the headmaster that the yawning stopped. By that time it was the end of the geography lesson, and Mr. Emsworth came in to teach them Scripture.

"I'm afraid you'll find them very naughty and inattentive to-day, Mr. Emsworth," Miss Lee said. "They're all yawning as if they were tired to death or else bored to tears. I've never met anything like it in my life before."

Mr. Emsworth said cheerfully that of course they couldn't be bored with her lesson, and then quietly began his own. Miss Lee retired to her desk and began correcting exercise books, and Jack tried hard to keep his mind on what the curate was saying.

However, it was no use. The words went on and on, but did not seem to make any sense. Presently he did not even hear the words, for his head went down on his desk and he was fast asleep.

How long he slept he did not know, but he was jerked back to wakefulness suddenly by Miss Lee's high, indignant voice.

"Jack Godden! Tony Brew! How dare you! Wake up at once."

Jack jerked his head up, to see her standing

close beside him. She was shaking Tony's shoulder, and he was grumbling and mumbling as though he were in bed at home. Mr. Emsworth, who had not realized why Miss Lee had suddenly left her desk and flown down the classroom, now followed her.

"All right, Miss Lee; I'll deal with this."

"I'm sorry," said Jack, but his eyes were on the curate as he spoke, and this further irritated Miss Lee.

"I insist on an explanation. Jack—were you late in bed last night, that you can't keep your eyes open to-day?"

Jack crimsoned, and Tony woke up at last with a mighty yawn that made the whole class laugh. Then a boy sitting in the back row piped up with an explanation.

"They was stowaways last night, miss."

"What's that?" Miss Lee whirled round to face the speaker, sure that someone was trying to make a fool of her.

"They was, miss," someone else assured her. "They stowed away on board o' their fathers' boat, the *Mary Uden*. They didn't come home till cock-crow, or thereabouts."

"Is this true?" demanded Miss Lee, turning to Tony and Jack again.

"Yes, miss," said Jack miserably, and Tony grunted.

"I never heard of such a thing. Did your fathers know?"

"No, miss."

"Of all the bad, naughty boys! Well, I must

say I'm surprised. Surely I've seen you both going to Sunday School? I'm surprised that boys who go to Sunday School, and in Mr. Emsworth's class too, I believe, should do a thing like that. I should have thought you'd be above that sort of thing."

Now Mr. Emsworth thought it time to interfere, and touched her firmly on the arm.

"Oh, no," he said serenely. "Boys don't get to be saints all of a sudden just because they go to Sunday School, even in my class, Miss Lee. Even grown-up people are not all saints, you know. Boys who go to Sunday School try a bit harder than those who don't, but we all try and struggle, and we slip and rise again. But as long as we hold the Lord firmly by the hand, He'll pick us up when we fall, and He'll help us to do better next time. Remember that the Lord Jesus was a little boy once, and He knows that a boy can't go through life without getting into mischief sometimes. But the things that He does expect a boy to steer clear of, with His help, are telling lies, being unkind or dishonest—that sort of thing."

Miss Lee flounced back to her desk.

"Well, if you're on their side, Mr. Emsworth, I've nothing more to say, of course," she said.

"Yes, I'm on their side," he said, and all the class listened with astonishment. "Because I know the Lord is on their side, if they're on His. He loved children, boys and girls, and we have plenty of stories of Him in the Gospels telling of His love for children. He raised a little girl from the dead—can anybody tell me her name?"

All the class was silent, trying to think, and then a girl in the front row gave an answer.

"She didn't have a name, sir."

"Well, I expect she did, but we don't know it. We do know the name of her father though, don't we?"

Again the girl in the front row put up her hand. "Jairus, sir."

"That's right. Then there was a boy, if you remember, the only son of his mother. And then do you remember how the disciples tried to keep the children away from Jesus, thinking that He was tired. What did He say?"

This time it was Jack's hand that went up.

"Suffer the children to come unto Me——"

"That's right. Now here's a little point to remember. He did *not* say, 'Suffer the *good* children to come unto Me', did He?"

"No!" shouted the class.

"Exactly. He doesn't only want the good children, He wants them all. And He didn't ask if Jairus' daughter was a good little girl before he worked a miracle and brought her back to life. He loves all children, so never think that because you're naughty sometimes that He doesn't love you or doesn't want you. He does, just as much as He wants the good ones. What He wants is to know that you really are on His side, that you do love Him and that you will try to please Him. He doesn't expect you to be a saint all at once, but He will help you to be one by the time you are old. So never despair, keep on trying, and with His help you'll win in the end."

"Don't He mind, then, that Jack was a stowaway?" called a cheeky boy from the back of the classroom.

Mr. Emsworth looked thoughtful.

"What do you think about that, Jack? Did the Lord Jesus mind?"

Jack flushed.

"I suppose He must have done, 'cause Mum was worried," he said slowly.

The curate nodded.

"Yes, you're right. Well, I expect you've put that right by now, and I'm not going to ask you any more questions about it. It isn't anybody else's business, though if you'd like to talk to me about it any time, you know where to find me. Now my time's up, so I'll say good-bye. Good morning, Miss Lee."

Jack did fairly well for the rest of the day, and did not fall asleep again during school hours. But something that Mr. Emsworth had said stuck in his mind, and after tea he determined to find him. He gave Tony the slip, not particularly wanting to have him around during the conversation that he was planning, and turned up at the curate's lodgings a minute after that busy man had come in late to his tea.

"I don't know that you can see him," said the landlady who opened the door. "He's only just this instant moment come in for his tea, and he was out half the night, so he must be dog-tired. Is it very important?"

"Not very," said Jack, and turned away down-cast. But Mr. Emsworth had heard voices, and now came to the door with a piece of bread-and-butter in his hand.

"Someone for me, Mrs. Newman? Oh, hullo, Jack. Come in. Had your tea?"

"Yes, sir. But I'd better not disturb you——"

"You're not disturbing me. You don't mind if I go on eating while you talk, do you? Come in and sit down. Have a piece of cake. Mrs. Newman makes jolly fine cakes. Now, what did you want to see me about?"

Jack squirmed rather uneasily on his chair, a piece of plum cake in his hand.

"Well, sir, I wanted to say I was sorry for keeping you out all night. I never thought anything like that would happen—really I didn't."

"Of course you didn't—I knew that. I know you'd never do an unkind thing if you thought about it, Jack. It was just thoughtlessness, wasn't it? You thought what fun it would be to be a stowaway, but didn't think other people might be dragged into it."

"Yes, sir, that was it," said Jack.

"Well, that's all right then. Don't worry about it any more. A chap can't do more than say he's sorry in an affair like this, and we'll forget all about it now. Was that all you wanted to see me about?"

"No, sir. You—er—you said this morning, when I said I supposed the Lord Jesus did mind, because of it's worrying Mum, you said you expected I'd put that right already. What did you mean?"

"When we do something wrong," said the curate slowly, "there are two parts to it: we hurt somebody else, and we hurt the Lord Jesus. And both those parts have to be put right, if we really love the Lord and want to be on His side. You came to me and said you were sorry for keeping me out last night—well, that settled my side of it. I expect you said the same thing to your mother, didn't you?"

"Yes, sir, and I promised not to do it again."

"Good for you. Now we come to the other part; through worrying your mother, you hurt the Lord, Who loves her as He loves you. Have you put it right with Him?"

"Well, sir, when I said my prayers this morning, I said 'Forgive us our trespasses'."

"It's a good idea, when you say that, to stop for a minute and think of anything special that needs forgiveness. Or to say another prayer afterwards confessing anything that you know has been wrong. Otherwise it's awfully easy to rush through the Lord's Prayer, thinking about something else all the time—isn't it?"

Jack flushed. Sometimes he managed to think about what he was saying when he said "Our Father", and sometimes he knew that he'd just rattled through it, thinking about something else, just as Mr. Emsworth said.

The curate laughed.

"All right, old boy—it happens to everyone now and then. Try to keep your mind on your prayers, and make them real talks with God, especially when confessing a wrong and asking for forgiveness. And always remember two very important things about that. One is that He *always* forgives when you honestly and humbly ask for pardon, and the other is that you must also put the matter right with the person you have wronged, too."

"Yes, sir," said Jack.

"You see what I mean, don't you? For instance, if a boy steals something from Woolworth's—no, I know you wouldn't do that, Jack, but it's awfully easy in those places where the things are laid out on the counter, and lots of boys do do it. Supposing a boy steals something like that—suddenly sees something he wants terribly badly, and yields to an impulse and slips it into his pocket. Then, when he's in bed that night, he realizes he's done wrong, and gets out of bed and kneels and asks God to forgive him. Well, that's perfectly right, but there's something else he's got to do, isn't there?"

"He's got to give the thing he stole back to the shop," said Jack.

"Yes, and that's the difficult part. Some people find it fairly easy to confess their sins to God, but not to the person they've done wrong to. But the two things must go together. Always remember that, won't you, Jack?"

"Yes, sir," said Jack. He got up to go. "Thank you very much, sir. And thank you for the cake, too. Good-night."

He felt very much happier as he went home.

Chapter 7

THE SAND-CASTLE COMPETITION

SCHOOL was over, and the summer holidays had begun. All Hythe was plastered with posters advertising two forthcoming attractions— a Fair to be held on the recreation ground in a week's time, and a sand-castle competition at Dymchurch, run by the *Daily Post*, on the first Saturday of the holidays.

Jack noticed both these posters, of course, and so did most of the other children in the town. Tony and Betty were full of excitement about it.

"It says First Prize, Three pounds," said Tony. "We ought to go and try our luck, Jack. If we win the first prize, we could save it up for the Fair. How many swings could you have for that?"

Betty did a rapid sum in her head.

"Twenty," she said.

"Coo!" Tony's eyes grew round with excitement. "Let's go. Jack, would your mum let you go?"

"I'll ask her," said Jack. "She might give us the bus fare. Or we could walk."

"It's five miles by road," said Betty.

"Yes, but it's not as far along the sea wall," said Jack. "I'll go and ask my mum, and you ask yours. Go on—hurry."

Neither of the mothers saw any objection to the plan, and Mrs. Godden suggested that they should take sandwiches with them and make a day of it. She also said she would pay their fares one way if Mrs. Brew would pay them on the return journey, and so it was arranged. The money was given to Betty to look after, but Jack carried the food in a haversack on his back, because boys always carry the loads. Tony carried nothing, but he offered to take a spell with the haversack later on if Jack got tired.

When they arrived in Dymchurch they saw great banners all across the road, with the name of the *Daily Post* on them in big red letters, and the sand-castle competition in big blue letters. Crowds of children were streaming up on to the wall, and they all carried buckets and spades. But Jack had brought a piece of wood that he rather fancied for doing sand work, and Tony had his mother's kitchen shovel, while Betty had a garden trowel.

The tide was right out when they got there, and that meant that there was a tremendous expanse of sand. The water was three-quarters of a mile away, some of them said, and the sands were golden and firm, just lovely for modelling.

There were several men and women who seemed to be in charge, the men wearing rosettes on their shirts with the name of the *Daily Post* in red on them, and the women wearing sashes marked in the same way. The sands were divided off into squares, and every competitor was given a square to work in. Jack thought that someone had been pretty busy that morning, marking off all those squares.

When everyone was settled a big, fat man stood up on a little platform, and told them the rules. Actually there did not seem to be any rules, except the one that they must not argue with the judges. They could make anything they liked, they could start as soon as he blew his whistle, and they must stop at twelve o'clock, when he would blow his whistle again. Then they must sit by the thing they had made until the judges came round and looked at it.

That seemed fairly simple, and Jack was only too anxious for the whistle to blow and let him begin. He knew exactly what he wanted to make —a model of the *Mary Uden*. As soon as the whistle went he began heaping up the sand for the first outline of his beloved ship.

Now Jack was a seaman born and bred, and he knew all the little bits and pieces about a fishing-boat that ordinary people would not notice. He knew how long she ought to be, and how broad; he knew how high the sides were and just about where the hatch-cover over the hold must go. He knew how high the slender, tapering mast must be, in comparison with the length and breadth of the boat, and he knew how many lines of rigging he would have to mark out on the sand.

Of course he made his model much smaller than the real boat, and he had to make a sideways view of her, lying on the sand, because he could not have got a sand mast to stand up, much less sand ropes. But he made it look just right, all the same, and as he worked he forgot all about the competition and everything, because he was enjoying himself so much.

Tony had quite a different idea. Aeroplanes were Tony's passion, and he had quite a good collection of toy ones at home. Now he thought he would make an aeroplane, and set to work cheerfully with the kitchen shovel that his mother had not missed yet, and made the finer parts with his fingers and a piece of shell.

Betty cared nothing for ships or aeroplanes, but she loved animals. Once, at a travelling circus, she had seen a tiger in a cage, and now she determined to make a model of the tiger striding up and down, as she had seen him on that occasion. And so she started work too, and all around were children making castles, houses, ships, aeroplanes, dogs, horses, gardens, and everything you can think of.

From time to time the men and women in their rosettes and sashes walked round to see how everyone was getting on. They said kind, encouraging words to the youngest ones, and sometimes called each other to come and look at something that particularly caught their fancy. But they did not stop very often by Jack, or Tony or Betty, and it looked as though they did not think their models very interesting.

Suddenly the whistle blew, and Jack looked up in great surprise, having quite forgotten why he was making the model of his beloved *Mary Uden*. Then he saw all the children round him stopping work, and remembered. He grinned and stopped too.

The man on the platform began to speak to them again, and said they could have another ten minutes for finishing off. Everyone breathed a great sight of relief, and began at once to put those finishing touches that their work needed. Betty put in the tiger's whiskers with seaweed, but they would not stick and she nearly cried about it. Tony thought his aeroplane was good enough for any number of first prizes, and sat back with a smile, waiting for the judges to come and look at it. Jack put the last finishing touches to his boat and, when the whistle blew for the second time, he was satisfied that the model was as good as he could make it.

The judges began to walk round. They stopped for a minute or two by Tony's aeroplane, and said a few nice things about it, and they quite admired Betty's tiger because it looked so fierce. But they did not think very much of Jack's boat.

One of the women in coloured sashes said that she thought it showed very little imagination.

"It's just an *ordinary* boat," she said. "Why didn't you make a battleship or a galleon, if you wanted to make a ship? You know—nice, spreading sails for a galleon—like Drake had against the Spanish Armada—or lots of guns for a battleship."

"It's the *Mary Uden*," said Jack. "My dad's boat. He goes out every night fishing in her."

"Yes, but it's so plain. Why didn't you put a flag in the front?" asked the woman.

"The *Mary Uden* hasn't got a flag in the front," said Jack. "Ships have their flags at the back, anyway."

"Oh, no, my dear," said the woman, and went away laughing. Jack turned to Tony.

"She doesn't know anything about it," he said.

"Not a bit," said Tony. "That's a funny thing; I thought grown-ups knew everything."

"I thought everyone knew that ships didn't have a flag at the front," said Jack. "I've seen lots and lots of ships, so I ought to know. Sometimes they have one at the top of the mainmast, but they always have one at the back—that is, if they're the sort of ships that have flags. The *Mary Uden* isn't, that's all."

"Well, you won't get a prize, that's certain," said Tony. "She liked my aeroplane, but she didn't seem to know much about it. She asked if it was a bomber. A bomber!" repeated Tony with derision. "I said it was a Miles Messenger passenger plane, like the one up at Lympne, and she seemed disappointed. I told her it ought to be blue, and she said she supposed that would make all the difference."

The judges were coming round again, and all the children watched them expectantly. Presently there was a burst of cheering, and the first prize had been given to a girl who had made a model of Westminster Abbey—and a very fine model it was, too. Then there was more cheering, and the second prize went to Betty for her tiger. Some people thought she ought to have had the first prize, because her tiger was so good, but most of them said the model of the Abbey was best, and so she got second prize. The third prize went to a boy who made a picture of Sir Winston Churchill.

Second prize was two pounds. Betty was rather disappointed that she had not got more. However, two pounds was something, and then Tony was given a consolation prize of twenty-five pence, to his great delight, which meant that they now had two pounds twenty-five to take them to the Fair next week.

When all the judging was over, the children strolled about looking at the other models. Jack said quite honestly that he thought the model of Westminster Abbey really deserved the first prize, it was so good. He did not know it was the Abbey because he had never been to London and had never seen it, but it was a lovely model of a fine, big church, anyway, and he went all round it and looked at it from every side, and told the girl who had made it that he thought she was jolly clever.

"Can I see yours?" asked the girl, who wanted to say something polite in return for Jack's remarks, so he took her round to see the *Mary Uden*. And then a surprising thing happened, for the girl knew a lot about boats too—her father had a sailing-boat and often took her out in it, and she knew about ropes and cleats and all sorts of things that the judges had never heard of. So she admired Jack's boat, and went all round it and looked at it from every angle too, and they talked about boats for a long time.

Then it was dinner-time, and most of the children went home. Jack and Betty and Tony had theirs on the top of the sea wall, and then went down to paddle and play about on the beach before starting for Hythe.

Mr. and Mrs. Godden wanted to know how Jack had got on at the competition, and were highly amused when he said that the lady judging his boat didn't know anything about boats at all.

"So you didn't get a prize, eh?" said Mr. Godden teasingly. "I expect you put everything back to front—and then blame it on the poor soul who was judging."

"I wish you'd come and look at it, Dad," said Jack. "It's neap tide this evening—the sea won't come anywhere near the models. Do come—can't you?"

"You could ride in on your bike," said Mrs. Godden.

"And take me on the carrier," said Jack. "Oh, do, Dad!"

So Mr. Godden said that he would, and as soon as tea was over he brought out his bicycle, and they set off to ride into Dymchurch again. They found that the tide was coming in fast, but it was a neap tide, as Jack had said, which means a tide that does not come in as far as usual—just as a spring tide means one that comes up much higher than usual—and so although a good many of the models were flattened by the waves, Jack's boat was untouched, although the waves were coming very near to it.

"Well," said Mr. Godden, walking round the

boat and looking at it professionally, "I think that's a very good boat indeed. Maybe that after hatch is a bit too far aft, but not much. Not enough to matter, anyway. I think you ought to have got a prize for that."

"Well, the prizewinners were better really," said Jack. "Specially the one of a big church—I forget its name, but it was super. I'm afraid it's under the sea now, but I wish you could have seen it."

"Is that Tony's aeroplane?" asked Mr. Godden. "Looks to me like the one that comes over from Lympne sometimes."

"That's the one it's supposed to be," said Jack triumphantly. "And here's Betty's tiger—well, the sea has washed its tail away, but most of it's here. It looks awfully fierce, doesn't it?"

"So she got second prize for that, did she?" said Mr. Godden. "I reckon you ought to have got something for your boat, then. But you say the lady said you ought to have put guns and flags and sails on it, eh?"

"So she said," said Jack scornfully.

"Do you wish now that you'd put some of those things on the *Mary Uden*, and won some money?" asked his father.

Jack pondered the matter.

"No," he said at last. "No, I don't. The *Mary Uden* is the *Mary Uden*, and if I started putting flags and guns on her, it wouldn't be the *Mary Uden* at all, would it?"

"You're quite right," said his father. "And I'll tell you another thing: you always do things the best you can, and then you needn't mind what people say. That lady now, she didn't know you'd made this boat just right, to the best of your ability, but there's Someone knows whenever we do our best, and gives us credit for it. You know that, don't you?"

"Do you mean that *you* know when a thing's right?" asked Jack, a bit puzzled by his father's words.

"No, I don't mean me—I mean Someone else."

"Jesus?" asked Jack.

"That's right," said his father. "Our Lord likes to see a job of work properly done, even if it's a small thing and not important to anyone else. St. Paul once said: 'Whatsoever thy hand findeth to do, do it with thy might, as unto the Lord'. I reckon when the Lord Jesus was a boy and worked in the carpenter's shop with His brothers, He did the jobs properly. Joseph didn't have to come to Him and say, 'Now that's a slip-shod piece of work—do it again.' He'd do it right first time, because He naturally liked to see things done right. So even if I hadn't come along and said your boat was a good job well done, the Lord has seen it, and you can thank your stars you put your best work into it, because He knows all about boats too."

"He knows everything, doesn't He, dad?" asked Jack.

"Yes, He does, but I like to think He knows about boats rather special," said Ben Godden the fisherman, "because he sailed on the Sea of Galilee with fishermen too."

Chapter 8

THE FAIR

JACK thought that he had lost his chance of going to the Fair, as he had not won a prize in the sand-castle competition. He did not like to ask his mother for some money again, so soon after she had paid their fare into Dymchurch and given them their dinner to take with them. So he said no more about it, but he did feel a bit glum when he heard the music of the merry-go-rounds blaring out, and saw most of the children he knew hurrying off down the road towards the recreation ground.

He was just making up his mind that he would spend the afternoon in the shed, making something, when he heard a cooee from the other side of the wall, and Tony's face peeped over.

"Doing anything this afternoon?" asked Tony.

"No," said Jack.

"What about coming to the Fair?" asked Tony.

Jack turned very red, thinking that Tony was pulling his leg.

"I can't," he said.

"Why not?" asked Tony. Then his foot slipped on the box he was standing on, and he disappeared from sight.

"That's settled him," thought Jack, and began to march down the path towards the shed.

However, before he had gone many steps he heard the cooee again, and there was Tony, sitting on top of the wall this time.

"Why can't you come to the Fair?" asked Tony.

"Because I haven't got any money. I didn't win any prizes," growled Jack.

"Oh, that doesn't matter," said Tony airily. "Betty and me have pooled our winnings, and we want you to come too."

Jack stared at him in growing delight.

"Do you mean it?" he asked.

"Course we do. We've got £2.25," said Tony. "It costs fifteen pence to go in, so that's forty-five pence—isn't it? Betty says it is, and she does money sums at school."

"Yes, it's forty-five pence," said Jack, after counting it out on his fingers.

"Well, that leaves ever such a lot for swing-boats and roundabouts," said Tony. "More than one pound, doesn't it?"

Again Jack did some sums with his fingers.

"One pound eighty," he said. "But you ought to be able to work that out for yourself."

"I'm not good at sums," said Tony. "Well, are you coming?"

"I'll just ask Mum," said Jack, and dashed indoors to get permission to go to the Fair.

Mrs. Godden thought it was very kind of Tony and Betty to invite Jack to go with them to the Fair, so she cut a few slices of currant cake for them to take with them. Jack rushed out and joined the other two, who were waiting for him and swinging on the front gate at the same time.

"If we got under the ropes, we needn't pay to go in," said Betty.

Jack felt very uncomfortable.

"I'd rather not do that. Dad wouldn't like it," he said. "I'll go home if you'd rather—I don't mind a bit."

"I don't see why you want to bother about what your dad likes when he isn't here. No one's going to tell him, if you do climb through the ropes," said Betty crossly.

Jack wondered how he could explain that it was because he loved his father that he did not like to do things he wouldn't like, but it was too difficult to put into words and he just shrugged his shoulders.

"Well, we're going to try," said Betty defiantly.

"O.K.," said Jack, pretending he did not care. "I'll sit here a bit and watch the people go in."

Tony and Betty ran off, and went all round the enclosure trying to find a way in without being seen. They thought they had found one once, but Tony was half-way through when a big man came up from nowhere and pounced on him, and gave him a good spank on the seat.

"That'll teach you to try and get into places without paying," he growled. He glared at Betty, who was out of reach. "I'd give you one too, for two pins," he said.

Jack was just a bit surprised when his two friends suddenly appeared again, still outside the enclosure.

"Come on, Jack," said Tony, trying to look as though nothing had happened, and Jack thought he had better not ask questions. So they all three went up to the entrance and Betty paid the money, and in another moment they were inside with all the exciting things going on all around them.

"Swings!" cried Tony, and began to run. The others dashed after him, and they joined a group of children waiting for a turn on the swing-boats. Presently it was their turn, and Jack and Tony pulled so hard on the ropes that it almost looked as though the boat was going to turn right over the top of the stand, and Betty held on tightly and shrieked. Then the man shouted to them to go more carefully, and soon their turn was over.

They went on a roundabout next. Jack sat in a funny seat shaped like a swan, with Betty on the seat opposite to him, but Tony found one that was made like an aeroplane, and of course he chose that. They went round and round, and up and down, and it seemed to go on for ever. And then suddenly it stopped, and Betty protested at the top of her voice that it was ever such a short go—much shorter than the other children had had.

"Let's buy some lemonade," said Tony. "I'm thirsty."

"I've got some cake," said Jack, remembering what it was that made his pocket stick out so uncomfortably.

"All right," said Betty. "We'll have lemonade and cake. Wait a tick and I'll go and buy some."

When she came back she was looking rather blank.

"That's all our money gone," she said. "It was thirty pence a bottle and I got one each."

"You must have lost some," said Tony accusingly.

"No, it's all right," said Jack sadly. "It cost 45p to go in, 45p for the swing-boats and 45p for the roundabout and 90p for the lemonade. That's two pounds twenty-five. And you only had two pounds twenty-five."

"I thought we were going to have lots and lots of rides," grumbled Tony. He munched his cake thoughtfully. "What can we do now?"

"Oh, there's plenty to see," said Jack. "We can hang about and watch."

"Someone might treat us," said Betty hopefully.

"This is jolly good lemonade, anyway," said Jack.

"So's the cake," said Betty politely.

Tony said nothing. He was thinking that all his money had gone very quickly.

They soon finished their refreshments and began to wander round the Fair again. They had not really seen round it yet, as they had dashed first to the swings and then to the roundabout when they first went in. Now they wandered among the stalls, and presently found themselves near a place where people were rolling pennies down a board to try and get them on to coloured squares. If their penny fell on the right square the man behind the stall had to give them fifty pence, or a pound, or even five pounds, according to what was marked on the lucky square.

A man was standing there as they watched, rolling down penny after penny, but none of them fell on a marked square so he lost them all. He was getting crosser and crosser, and suddenly turned round and saw the children watching him.

"Here, you," he said to Jack. "Come and roll this penny down for me. Perhaps you'll change my luck. I'll give you half whatever I win, if you do."

But Jack backed away.

"I'd rather not," he stammered.

"Why not? Come along—I shan't eat you," said the man roughly. "I'll give you half my winnings—word of honour."

"I can't," said Jack, going crimson. "Dad says it's gambling, and I promised I wouldn't."

"I will! I will, sir," cried Tony, rushing forward, but the man was looking curiously at Jack, and took no notice of him.

"So your dad says it's gambling, does he?" he asked.

"Yes, sir," said Jack.

"And he won't let you gamble?"

"No, sir."

"Is he here?"

"No, sir," said Jack.

"Well, don't you want to try your hand at it? You might be lucky," said the man.

"Well, sir," said Jack apologetically, hoping the man would not think him rude, "it does seem to be a bit of a mug's game. I mean—you keep on losing your pennies. I don't see the sense of it."

"Yes, but you see I might win five pounds," said the man. "Don't you think it's worth risking a few pennies to win five pounds?"

"If it was something I could practise up and get good at, it would be different," said Jack. "But however clever you are, you can't make the pennies go differently."

"It's pure chance," agreed the man. "That's what makes it so fascinating."

"Dad says that's what makes it wrong," objected Jack.

"I'll do it, sir," pleaded Tony, tugging at the man's sleeve. "Let me do it for you, sir. My dad doesn't say it's wrong, and I wouldn't care if he did. I'd do it to oblige you, sir, whatever he said."

"Run away," said the man. "Can't you see I'm talking to someone?"

Tony drew back, and the man turned to Jack again.

"Do you never do anything your dad thinks wrong?" he asked.

Jack flushed again, and kicked the ground.

"I suppose I do, sometimes," he muttered.

"But, on the whole, you don't, eh? You must be very fond of your dad, old man."

Jack raised his eyes, surprised by the sudden friendliness in the man's voice.

"Yes, I am," he said. "He's the best father in the world."

"I had a good father too," said the man, moving slightly away from the counter where more people were now rolling pennies down the board and losing them. "And I used to like to do what pleased him. But since I've been grown-up, I'm afraid I've forgotten a bit. He didn't like gambling either, and I made him a promise once to have nothing to do with it. You've reminded me. Thanks."

Jack felt rather embarrassed at these words, and grinned a bit shyly.

"I expect he's been dead a long time," he said politely.

"Well, as a matter of fact, he has," said the man. "Now, what about a ride on the swings—eh?"

"Actually, we've used up all our money," said Jack. "That's why we were watching you. We're together, you see—Betty and Tony and me. They won some prizes at the sand-castle competition in Dymchurch last week, and I didn't win anything, so they asked me to come with them as they're my friends. And we've been on the swings and the roundabout, and we had some lemonade, and that finished all our money."

"Well, I expect I could stand treat a bit," said the man. "Particularly as I'm not going to gamble on the penny board any more. What would you like to do? See if you can win anything at shooting? That's not gambling, you know."

"Oh, no, that's all right, but I can't shoot," laughed Jack.

"I'll show you how it's done," said the man promptly, and for the next half-hour they had lots of fun while he taught them all to shoot.

He was awfully clever at it himself, and hit the target every time, and the man who looked after the guns and took the money said he was a wonder. But Jack could not hit the target at all, and when Betty did it once everyone said it was an accident. Still, they enjoyed it very much, and were quite sorry when he said at last that he would have to go now.

He shook hands with them all, and they remembered to thank him. Then he gave them each fifty pence, and they had to thank him again. At last he turned to Jack with a smile.

"I like your pluck, my lad," he said, "and I've thoroughly enjoyed this afternoon. I hope you never forget, as I did, the things you promise your dad when you're young."

"I'll try not to, sir," said Jack with a grin.

"That's right," said the man. "Good-bye, all."

They all waved good-bye to him as he went away, and then spent the rest of the time until they had to go home wondering how best to spend their money. In the end they had the last ride of the evening on the swings, and the man forgot they were there and let them go on for a long, long time—to their great joy. Altogether it was a most successful visit.

Chapter 9

A LITTLE HARD WORK

THE day after the visit to the Fair dawned bright and sunny, and it was a little sad to think that the three friends had no money left, and could not go again. The Fair was there for three days, but as far as Jack and Tony and Betty were concerned, it might just as well go away at once. The sound of its music, and the puffing of the big engine that drove the roundabouts and things, was just an annoyance to those who could not go again. Jack remembered the joys of the previous day, and sighed.

"Like to dig me some bait, son?" called Mr. Godden from the kitchen door.

Jack, who was busy in his shed, looked up at once.

"Right-ho, Dad. How much do you want?"

"I want quite a good bit; about three or four cans full. Several summer visitors came up to me when I was busy on the boat this morning, and asked if I could get them some bait. I told them to call round about six and I'd have some for them. Like to take the job on?"

"Rather," said Jack.

"They'll pay you for it," said his father.

"Thanks, dad," said Jack with a grin. "Then I can go to the Fair again."

"You can do what you like with the money," said his father.

"Can I get Tony and Betty to come along and help?"

"Yes, if you like. Find all the cans you can lay your hands on, and fill 'em all. I expect we shall have several folks here after bait if once it gets known I sell it," said Ben Godden.

Jack climbed up on to the wall that divided the two gardens, and cooeed for Tony. Presently his friend came out of the cottage, looking glum.

"What do you want?" he asked.

"Like to earn some money?" asked Jack.

Tony cheered up at once.

"How?" he asked.

"Digging for bait," said Jack.

Tony did not look quite so pleased.

"That's jolly hard work," he grumbled.

"Well, don't if you don't want to," said Jack. "I'm going to. We shall have to go to Dymchurch along the wall, because that's the nearest place. Tide will be about right soon, too. Are you coming? What about Betty?"

"I'll see what Betty says," said Tony, and disappeared indoors again.

Betty was full of enthusiasm for the idea. She never minded hard work, but Tony was inclined to be lazy. Betty found some tins and toy pails, and a sack to carry everything in, and a big spade, and said that she was coming.

"I might as well come too, then," said Tony reluctantly.

"You'll have to find your own tins, then," said Betty. "You can't have any of mine."

"You've got them all, greedy!" cried Tony.

"I'll help you find some," said Jack impatiently, and they hunted for a little while, and were at last ready to set off.

It did not take them very long to round the curve of the bay and reach the spot where numerous holes in the sand showed the existence of lug-worms. They began to dig, and little by little the tins filled up. Betty had brought far too many, of course, for it is rather a long, slow job, digging for bait. But she and Jack kept persistently at it, though Tony soon got tired, and went off to paddle and play in the sea.

Of course none of them had a watch, so they had to send Tony to ask the time every now and then. Tony complained, but Betty said that as he was not digging he must do something else to help. Jack meant to get home well before six, so as not to miss any of the intending purchasers, and at last he gave the word to pack up their spades and tins and return.

"But I haven't filled half my tins," objected Betty.

"Can't be helped," said Jack. "We'll come again to-morrow, and dig some more. Then we'll have lots of money for the last day of the Fair."

They were very lucky, for on their way home two or three people stopped them and asked if they might buy some bait. Tony began to think he might be going to be left out of a good thing, and sidled up to Jack wheedlingly.

"I did help a bit, didn't I? I did ask the time for you too. You'll share with me, won't you?

I did take you to the Fair yesterday when you hadn't any money."

"All right," said Jack rather impatiently. "Of course we'll take you with us. What d'you take me for? Shut up!"

They got back in time to hand the tins over to Mr. Godden, who arranged the amounts each tin was to hold, and told them how much they could charge. Jack told his father that they had sold some on the return journey from the sands, and he nodded.

"I wonder you boys don't do more of that," he said. "There's lots of people in the summer season only too anxious to buy bait. You could make a tidy bit of money if you liked."

"Too much like work for me," said Tony cheerfully.

"Lazy little blighter!" cried his sister.

Jack and Betty went out the following day to dig for more bait, but Tony did not go with them. He said he was tired. But when they returned and added together all the money they had made he was not tired at all.

"Are you ready to go?" he asked anxiously.

"I've got to wash first," said Jack. "My hands are all mucky."

"I've lost my hair-clip," said Betty. "Wait for me while I see if Mum's got one for me."

"You'll have to wash too," said Jack. "You're dirtier than I am."

"Oh," said Betty, looking doubtfully at her hands. "All right. I do think you're fussy, though."

"Oh, hurry up!" cried Tony, dancing with impatience. "The Fair will be over before you two are ready."

They got there at last, and had a wonderful time. They had to leave before the end, of course, and even so they were late in for bed. But just before they left an old man beckoned to Jack.

"We pack up to-morrow morning, son," he said. "Like to come and give us a hand? There's plenty to do."

"Rather!" said Jack. "Can I bring my friends?"

"If you're sure they won't pinch anything," said the old man. "I asked you 'cause you look as if you'd got an honest face. We don't want all sorts here."

Jack said that he was sure Betty and Tony were honest, and ran after them to tell them what the man had said. They were highly excited about it; and arranged that whoever woke up first next morning should wake the other two, and that they should set off at the earliest possible moment.

Strangely enough, it was Tony who woke first. He knocked up Betty; then they both dressed and tip-toed downstairs, and threw stones at Jack's window to wake him. One of the stones went straight through the open window instead of rattling on the glass, and hit Jack on the nose. He woke up in a towering rage, and rushed to the window to shake his fist at them and tell them exactly what he thought of them for such behaviour.

Of course they did not know what all the fuss

was about. They did not know that the stone had hit him on the nose, and Betty got quite indignant with him.

"You asked us to call you, and now you make a fuss about it," she said sharply. "All right—you can call yourself another time."

"I only said throwing stones was a silly trick," said Jack.

"How else did you expect us to wake you? Knock at the door?" asked Betty sarcastically.

"You hit me on the nose," said Jack with great dignity, but the result was not what he expected, for they both broke into shrieks of stifled laughter. "I think you're pigs," he said definitely. "I'll be down in a minute."

When they reached the Fair, great activity was going on. The men were taking down stalls and packing them up, and the women were cooking breakfast. Jack, Tony and Betty suddenly remembered that they had come out without having their breakfast, and felt very empty. The frying bacon smelled so good that their mouths watered. However, the old man who had spoken to Jack soon gave them jobs to do, and although they gazed longingly at the food from time to time, no one seemed to think that they needed any.

They worked really very hard for a long time, piling wooden trestles into a huge van, and then one of the women called Betty to her.

"Will you mind Baby for me, love? He crawls into the fire if I leave him by himself, and I want to help my Joe with the stall."

"All right," said Betty obligingly. Then her eye caught half a loaf lying on the ground. "Do you think I might have a little bit of bread?" she asked. "We came out before Mum was up, and we didn't have any breakfast."

"Why, you poor little things!" cried the woman. "Look here—cook yourselves some bacon while you mind Baby. No, more than that, love—two good rashers each. You'll find some eggs in there, too. And some butter for your bread. Call the boys and have a good meal, love—you can't work if you're empty inside."

So Betty joyfully called the boys, and Tony played with the baby while Jack buttered the bread and Betty cooked the bacon and eggs. Jack said the food came along just in time to save his life, but Tony said he couldn't do any more work because he was too full up!

It was ten o'clock before the Fair was ready to move, and then all the tractors and lorries and caravans moved slowly off the recreation ground in a long string, and joined the main Dymchurch road. Perched high on the first great gaily-painted pantechnicon that held the swing-boats were the three children, the envy of all their friends. Traffic was held up, people stood on the pavements and waved and cheered, and the Fair moved on to New Romney, ten miles or so along the road.

About a mile outside Hythe the procession came to a halt, and Jack, Tony and Betty climbed down. They said good-bye to their new friends and wished them luck, and then hurried home, wondering if they were going to be late for dinner. They were quite surprised when their mothers said that it would be another hour to dinner-time; they thought they had been up for ages!

Chapter 10

THE MISSION

"WHAT'S going on over there?" ejaculated Tony.

The other two stared in the direction of his pointing finger. The tide was low, and quite a number of children were gathered round a big flag on which some words were printed in very big letters.

"Let's go and see," said Jack. From all over the beach children were going towards the big flag; some slowly and shyly and some rushing eagerly. A man and a woman seemed to be giving out something, but they could not see what it was.

"It's a mission," said Jack suddenly, as the wind caught the big flag and spread it out so that they could see the words on it.

"What's a mission?" asked Tony.

"Oh . . . sort of religious . . ." said Jack vaguely. "Like Sunday school only strangers come and talk. We had one in our church once."

"Oh!" said Tony, deeply disappointed. "How do you know? It might not be."

"Well, didn't you see what it said on the flag just now?" asked Jack.

"I did," said Betty. "Something about children coming to him . . . suffering children or something. Perhaps he's a doctor."

Jack felt rather important because he knew the text on the flag, and his friends did not.

"It says: 'Suffer the children to come unto Me'," he said. "Jesus said that. So it's bound to be a mission. Come on . . . there'll be hymns and things, and it might be fun."

"You've got funny ideas of fun," growled Tony, but he followed Jack, and they all reached the edge of the crowd round the flag in time to hear the young man who seemed to be in charge of it play a few bars on a very funny little organ. The sound of the organ interested Tony, and he squeezed in through the crowd to get a look at it. It was very small, and had handles on the side so that it could be carried. The man was sitting on a camp stool, working the pedals with his feet and playing over the first verse of a hymn.

"Now then," he said when he had come to the end of it, "you've all got books, haven't you?"

"I haven't," said Tony.

"Susie—here's a young man without a book," said the man, and a nice-looking young woman came up to Tony with a red-backed hymn-book.

"Any more?" she asked, waving them in the air, and several newcomers, including Jack and Betty, asked for one.

"Ready now?" asked the man. "All together: 'Tell me the stories of Jesus . . .' "

They all sang heartily; many of the children knew the old hymn very well, and the man played the organ as though he were enjoying himself very much. The girl he had called Susie had a nice voice, and sang loudly, so it went with a swing. Jack was quite sorry when they reached the end of it.

The man then got up from his camp stool and asked them to close their eyes in prayer. Then he asked for God's blessing on their little service, and asked that a special message from God might be given to each one of the children listening. Then they all said "Our Father" together.

"Now we'll sing another hymn," said the man. "Anyone like to choose one?"

Several hands shot up at once, including Jack's, but the man pointed to a girl standing near-by.

"What's your choice?" he asked.

" 'All things bright and beautiful'," she said.

"That's a nice one," he said. "It is bright and beautiful to-day, isn't it? The sun is bright and the sea is beautiful. Can anyone tell me anything else that is bright and beautiful?"

A tiny little girl of about three or four was standing in front, listening intently. When he asked that question she knew the answer at once.

"Yes. Me!" she said promptly, and everyone laughed.

The man looked rather taken aback, for he had not expected that answer, but the girl came forward and kissed the little person who was so sure that she was bright and beautiful.

"Of course you are, darling," she said. "When little girls and little boys are good and happy, they are bright and beautiful. And when they love the Lord Jesus, they're good and happy, aren't they?"

"I've got a picture of the Baby Jesus in my bedroom," said the little girl. "With all the animals round His cot. And I say good-night to Him every night."

"That's splendid," said Susie. "Now shall we sing?"

So the man played over the tune, but then there was a chorus of interruptions.

"Oh, sir—we don't know that tune. That isn't our tune," cried half the children.

"Yes, that's our tune. We know that tune," cried the other half.

"What about this one?" asked the man, playing another melody on his organ.

But now the ones who had known the tune before cried out very loudly that they didn't know this one, and the others cried out that they did, and there was a thorough commotion.

"Quiet! Quiet!" cried the young man, and held up his hand. "Now I'll tell you what we'll do," he said when they had stopped arguing, "we'll sing it first of all in the first tune I played, and then we'll sing it again in the other tune. Then you'll all have learned a new tune, eh?"

So that is what they did. When it was finished the man read them something out of the Bible, and talked to them a little while. He talked so nicely that even Tony listened. He told them about the love of Jesus, Who came down from heaven to die on the cross for them, and told them that although He had gone up into heaven again, He still loved them and watched over them, and wanted them to love Him. Some of the children had never heard that before, and some had heard it but had not really listened, like Tony and Betty. And some, like Jack, knew it well but loved to hear about it all over again.

When he had finished talking they sang another hymn, and then the young man began to ask them questions. For some reason he pointed to Jack, and asked him what he was going to be when he grew up.

"A fisherman, like my dad," said Jack.

"A fisherman, eh? Well, I'm a fisherman too, of a sort. I wonder if you'd like to be my kind of fisherman?" asked the man.

Jack shook his head with a grin.

"I want to be like my dad," he said.

"That's fine, but I'll tell you the sort of fisherman I am, and then you'll see that you could be both kinds if you liked," said the man. "When the Lord Jesus was on earth he called two fishermen to follow Him, and said He would make them fishers of men. That's the sort of fisherman I am. Do you know what He meant?"

Nobody said anything for a moment; then Jack spoke.

"You catch men instead of fishes?" he asked uncertainly.

"That's right. I catch men for Christ. When a fisherman goes out to sea he throws out a net, and I throw out the Gospel net. But the difference is that when the fish swim into the net they're lost, but when men come into the Gospel net they're saved. And boys and girls too. It's never too early to give your heart to the Lord. I want you to think about that when you go to bed to-night. It's never too early, but one day it might be too late. Come to Him when you're young, and He will show you what He wants you to do with your lives. Now Susie and I will be here to-morrow evening too, and if any of you have thought about it, and made up your minds to come in on the Lord's side, come and tell me, will you?"

Some of the children murmured that they would, but most of them were too shy to say much. Then they sang another hymn, and the man ended the little service with the Blessing.

Most of the children ran away then, but Jack lingered. He liked the look of the young man, who was now packing up his organ.

"Can I give you a hand with that?" asked Jack shyly.

"Thanks very much, old man," was the friendly reply. "These straps are rather awkward. Hullo —where's Susie gone?"

"She's talking to the mother of the little kid who said she was bright and beautiful," chuckled Jack. "I say—would you come and have tea with us, sir? I'd like you to see my dad, and I'd like him to see you. You'd like him."

"I'm sure I should," said the man. "But what would your mother say about you bringing in strangers to tea?"

"Oh, she won't mind," said Jack. "She's a sport. And she knows all about the things you were talking about, too. She'd like it—honest, she would."

"Then I'd love to come," said the man. "Hi! Susie!" he shouted. "I've been invited out to tea."

"O.K.," called the girl, and went on talking to her new acquaintances.

"Is your home far?" asked the man. "I think we'd better dump this gear in the tents first. Will you give me a hand, as Susie seems to be occupied? We've got a couple of tents on the canal bank, and I think I'd like to park the organ and the flag, and have a wash, before I go out to tea."

"Do you live in a tent?" asked Jack as he helped to carry the organ along the road.

"Yes, in the summer. I only do this job in the summer holidays, you know. I live in London most of the year, and run a Sunday School and a boys' club and things like that, but in the summer Susie and I tour the seaside places with this mission."

"Is Susie your wife?" asked Jack.

"No, she's my young sister," laughed the man. "We both belong to an organization that sends out missioners . . . but you wouldn't understand about all that. That's how we spend our summer holiday, you see."

"It must be fun," said Jack, "going about all over the place."

"It is," was the answer. "But I'll tell you what's the best of all, and that is when young people we've been talking to about the Lord Jesus decide to follow Him and serve Him for the rest of their lives. Have you ever thought about it, old chap?"

"Well, yes," said Jack shyly. "Mr. Emsworth, that's our curate, you know, he talks about it pretty often, and—well, once when he'd been talking I thought I'd like to do it, and so I did that night when I said my prayers. I asked the Lord Jesus to take me on His side and help me to fight the devil. I meant it, too," he added.

"Shake hands!" said the young man, stopping and putting down his end of the portable organ. "We're both fishers of men really . . . you'll find that you want to help others to serve the Lord presently, and that's what the words mean. We're both on the same side. That's grand! Did you tell Mr. Emsworth what you'd done?"

"No," said Jack. "I didn't like to, somehow. Though he's awfully decent. I got into some trouble a little while ago, and he was awfully nice about it."

"I should tell him," said the man decidedly. "It'll please him no end. You tell him next time you get him alone. Now—here are the tents. Jolly, aren't they?"

Jack admired the two little tents tremendously. They were so trim and snug, with the camp gear looking neat and tidy, the primus stove and the kettle, frying-pan and small saucepan, the two cups and tin plates—everything looked most attractive.

"It's almost as good as a boat," said Jack, and the man roared with laughter.

"It's a great deal better than a boat for what we want," he said. "We cycle about, you know, and stop at villages all over the place, not only seaside places but quite inland. There's always someone who will lend us a field to put the tents up in, and we've often emptied one of them and used it as a tiny chapel when it's been raining. You'd be surprised how many people we can squeeze into one of these tents when we're holding a little service."

Jack thought it was delightful, and wandered about looking at everything while the man washed his face and hands, and combed his hair.

"There," he said at last, "I hope I'm tidy enough. Think I'll do?"

"You look super," said Jack. He looked at his own hands. "I'll wash when I get home," he said.

"You can wash here if you like," said the man, "in my patent folding camp washstand, guaranteed to fall over if you're not careful. Would you like to?"

Now that was exactly what Jack longed to do. Washing in the open air, in a green canvas bowl on funny lattice legs, struck him as a most amusing thing to do. When he was ready the man lent him his comb, and lowered the mirror on the tent-pole so that he could see to do his hair, and then at last they were ready to set off for the cottage and tea.

Chapter 11

A REAL MAN

"MUM, I've brought a new friend in to tea. He washed his face specially," cried Jack, bursting into the kitchen excitedly.

Mrs. Godden was just cutting the bread and butter, and her husband was playing with Baby Nellie. Thinking that Jack meant Tony or some other boy friend, she did not look up.

"Tell him to come in and sit down," she said cheerfully.

But Ben Godden, happening to glance up to smile a welcome, saw a tall form behind Jack's, and got to his feet.

"Good afternoon, sir," he said, holding out his hand.

Mrs. Godden looked startled and put down the knife.

"Well I never!" she exclaimed.

"I hope you don't mind," said the young man. "My name's Entwhistle—Tom Entwhistle, and I'm running a mission down on the beach. Jack came to our service this afternoon, and invited me to come back to tea with him afterwards. He said his mother wouldn't mind because she knew about the things we'd been talking about."

"That's right, sir," said Mrs. Godden heartily.

"Any servant of the Lord is welcome here. Sit down. Perhaps you'll say Grace for us, sir, as you're here?"

So Tom Entwhistle said Grace, and afterwards got busy on the good food. Mrs. Godden was secretly delighted that she had thought to make a cake that morning, and so had something nice to offer the visitor. However, he seemed quite happy eating her home-made jam, while Ben Godden talked to him about his work, and Jack sat listening, almost—but not quite—too excited to eat.

Young people are usually rather sensitive about discussing their spiritual experiences with those who know them best, and so Jack was glad that Mr. Entwhistle did not mention before Mr. and Mrs. Godden anything that he had told him. The talk was mostly about missions and a little about fishing, too, and everything was going well when there was a tap on the door and Mr. Brew came in.

"Come in, Brew," said Mr. Godden, although his wife did not look too well pleased. "This is my partner in the boat, Arthur Brew, sir. This is Mr. Entwhistle, who's running a mission down on the beach, Arthur."

Now when Mr. Brew came into the cottage, a great smell of drink came with him. He looked flushed, too, and irritable.

"He's got a headache," thought Jack. "Now for some fun!"

"Running a mission, eh?" said Mr. Brew rudely. "I should have thought a healthy young fellow like you could find a better job than that."

"Now, Arthur," said Ben Godden, rising to his feet, "you can't insult a guest in my cottage, you know."

"I don't mind," said Tom Entwhistle quietly. "I don't think there is a better job than mine, that's all."

"Well, it's not what I call a man's job," said Brew. "Let girls and women do that sort of thing if they must—keeps 'em occupied, perhaps. But a real man wants a real man's job, I say. A lot of use you'd be in a boat!"

"I don't suppose I should be much use, as I don't know anything about it," said Entwhistle.

"No, you take jolly good care to keep away from anything like that, don't you?" sneered Brew. "You wouldn't go where there's any danger— not you! I'd just like to see you in the *Mary Uden* one night. You'd howl to be put ashore."

"I don't think I should," said Tom Entwhistle.

"Come out with us to-night then—I dare you," said Brew offensively. "Oh, I know you can't come. You've got a mission on, I expect, and anyway the wind's rising and we're in for a dirty night. You'd best keep away from boats when there's a rising wind, young man. You'd soon howl to be set ashore, you would."

"I should be very glad of the opportunity to come," was the quiet reply, and Jack hugged himself with joy.

"If you mean that, sir, you'd be very welcome," said Ben Godden.

"I do mean it. What time do you set off?" asked Tom.

"Nine o'clock to-night," said Brew, looking surprised that his challenge had been accepted. "But you won't be there. The wind's rising, I tell you. We're in for a blow. You'll be seasick."

"Very probably," said Entwhistle. "But I'm coming. I'd like you to know that I can be about my Master's business and yet be what you call a real man."

"We never doubted that, sir," said Mr. Godden quickly.

"I know that, but Mr. Brew did. So I'll be down on the beach at ten to nine to-night."

Brew laughed scornfully, but said no more.

"What did you want to see me about, Arthur?" asked Mr. Godden.

"Nothing in particular. Just dropped in for a chat. As you've got company I won't intrude," said Mr. Brew, and took himself off. As a matter of fact Mrs. Brew had seen the stranger go into the Goddens' cottage with Jack, and she had persuaded her husband to go in and find out all about him. Mrs. Brew liked to know everything that went on around her, even when it was none of her business.

Now Mr. Brew went back and told her that the stranger was someone running a mission down on the beach.

"I told him what I thought of him," he said, "and dared him to come out with us to-night. He said he would, but I bet he doesn't. That sort doesn't care about getting wet and cold in a boat at sea. We shan't see him down there at nine o'clock."

Meanwhile Ben Godden was giving Tom Entwhistle a bit of advice.

"Have you got a good oilskin, sir? Brew's right when he says we're in for dirty weather to-night. Nothing to worry about, of course, but you'll get wet."

"I'm afraid I haven't got an oilskin or sea-boots or anything of that sort," said Entwhistle ruefully. "We're travelling light, for one thing."

"He could wear my sea-boots," said Mrs. Godden, laughing. "That is, if you wouldn't mind, sir. I only use them in the winter or when the weather's real bad. Try them on, and see if they fit."

"Your boots would never fit me," protested Entwhistle. "My feet must be miles bigger than yours."

"Oh, I've got mine extra big to go on over my slippers," said Mrs. Godden. "I don't think they'd fit otherwise."

So the missioner tried on Mrs. Godden's boots, and found that they fitted reasonably well. Mr. Godden had meanwhile gone down to the shed and found an old oilskin and sou'wester, which he could lend to their guest.

"Put on all the pullovers and coats you've got, underneath, sir," he advised. "You'll need 'em."

When Mr. Entwhistle took his leave, Jack ran up to his father and begged to be allowed to go too that night.

"It's holiday time, Dad, and I've never been to

sea on a dirty night, and Mr. Entwhistle is my
friend after all; I found him," pleaded Jack.

"What do you say, Mum?" asked Ben Godden.

"It's up to you, Dad," was the reply. "Don't
you think he'll get in the way?"

"Not him," said Ben Godden. "All right, son.
Get your boots and oilskin ready, and then go
and lie down till Mum calls you. You'll miss
a lot of sleep to-night, and you ought to get a bit
of a rest in before we go."

Jack did as he was told, and dropped off to
sleep at once. It seemed a very short time afterwards that his mother woke him up with a hot
cup of cocoa and some bread and dripping.

"Are you sure you want to go, son?" she asked.
"It's raining already, and blowing quite a bit."

However, Jack insisted that he wanted to go,
and drank the cocoa, put on his oldest and
warmest clothes, and hurried downstairs with the
bread and dripping in his hand, to join his father,
who was also getting ready.

They were joined by Mr. Brew at the gate,
and Jack noticed that the man's steps were
rather unsteady and that he seemed in a worse
temper than before. Very little was said, although
Brew swore at the weather from time to time,
until they reached the *Mary Uden* and found
Tom Entwhistle sheltering in her lee from the
driving rain.

"Oh, so you're here, are you?" grumbled
Brew. "I didn't think you'd come. Hadn't you
better change your mind and go home? You'll
get wet, you know."

"I probably shall," said Entwhistle.

"Then you'll catch a cold," sneered the other man.

"Very likely," said Entwhistle.

"Come along, Arthur, and give her a shove off," said Ben Godden sharply. "Hop aboard, Jack."

Jack jumped in over the side—more of a scramble than a jump—and the three men pushed the boat into the water. The waves were choppy and angry, and the boat jerked and pulled like a startled horse. Mr. Brew scrambled in next and ran forward to hoist the sail.

"In you go, sir," said Mr. Godden, holding the boat steady with an effort.

Entwhistle pulled himself up and fell aboard in rather an awkward fashion, and Brew found time from what he was doing to laugh sneeringly. Then Mr. Godden came neatly and cleanly aboard, the sail went up, and the *Mary Uden* danced away out into the bay.

Jack knew that there was nothing much he could do at this stage of the proceedings, so sat himself down quietly in the dryest spot he could find. Entwhistle, after hesitating a moment, sat down beside him.

"How d'you like it, sir?" asked Jack eagerly.

"It's too early to say," said Entwhistle cautiously. "Does it go up and down like this all the time?"

"This? This is nothing," laughed Jack. "Wait till we get outside the bay!"

Presently they could hear Brew, up in the

bows, swearing to himself as he worked on the nets.

"What's the trouble, Arthur?" called Mr. Godden from the stern.

"It's my head," was the reply, given with more bad language.

"Bad luck," said Mr. Godden, without much sympathy.

However, the head got worse, and presently Brew was lying down below, groaning, just at the time that his partner needed most help. However, Jack did all he could, and the missioner, although very unsteady on his feet in the boat, also helped, so the work was done.

"You're looking a bit green," said Mr. Godden bluntly after a while. "Like to go below, sir?"

Tom Entwhistle shook his head.

"No, I'll see it out. I'm feeling pretty green, I don't mind telling you, but I'll work it off, I think."

"Well, my old dad always did say that work was the best cure for seasickness," said Godden. "But you can go below if you like, sir."

But the missioner would not give in, and presently in the excitement of hauling up his first catch he forgot how ill he had been feeling, and worked enthusiastically. When they had settled down to cruising again he suddenly remembered, and laughed.

"What's the joke, sir?" asked Jack.

"I've lost my seasickness," said Entwhistle. "That's a joke, isn't it?"

Jack went below to the galley to make some

hot cocoa, and they ate some bread and cheese. Mr. Brew joined them for this repast, and scowled when he saw their visitor eating and drinking as heartily as any of them.

"Not laid out, then?" he asked sourly.

"Not a bit of it," said Mr. Godden cheerfully. "He's done your job for you to-night, Arthur. I reckon, that being the case, that you can't say he's anything but a real man, eh?"

When, hours later, they landed their catch through a tempestuous sea, Arthur Brew was bound, reluctantly, to admit that he was right.

Chapter 12

IN A SCRAPE AGAIN

LIFE was dull. The missioner and his sister had gone, the holidays were nearly over, and Jack complained that he had nothing to do. Being just an ordinary boy, he did not always remember that he had promised to follow the Lord Jesus all his life, and be on His side in the great fight between right and wrong. Sometimes he forgot that altogether, and he certainly had forgotten it when Betty Brew put up a grand suggestion for brightening up a dull day. It is always on dull days when we are bored that the devil comes along with his bright suggestions; when we are busy he cannot get his whispers through to us, and on this occasion he used Betty to tempt Jack into wrongdoing.

"Let's go to Dungeness on the baby train," said Betty.

The baby train, as she called it, was the Hythe to Dungeness light railway. The trains were very tiny—in fact if the driver stood up in one he towered out of the cab like a giant—and they pulled a line of four-seater carriages with open windows at a steady pace across the level Romney Marsh. Children all love the baby trains, and it is small wonder that Betty wanted a ride in one or that Jack's eyes brightened at her words. But the fact that they both ignored was that they had no money for a ticket.

"All right," said Jack recklessly. "What about Tony?"

"I'll call him out," said Betty, and did so at once.

"What's going on?" asked Tony.

"Hush!" said Jack. "We're going to Dungeness to see the lighthouse, on the baby train."

"Coo! What'll happen if we're caught?" asked Tony.

"I expect we'd go to prison, so we must make sure we're not caught," said Jack. "Come on . . . let's go." And they all three ran down the lane towards the main road that led to the station.

"I wonder which one will be in," said Tony as they trotted along. "I hope it's *Black Prince*."

"I hope it's *Green Goddess*," said Betty.

"Well, I hope it's *Enchantress*," said Jack. "We'll see who's right when we get there."

There was quite a crowd on the little station when they reached it, and the train standing puffing ready to go was the *Black Prince*. Tony was delighted—he had guessed right.

For a few minutes the three children hung about with the others as they moved slowly towards the booking office. There was not a chance of getting past the ticket inspector on the gate without a ticket—they knew that—so presently Jack gave a signal and darted back into the road again, and down the bank of the canal, which runs quite close to the line just there. They slid down the bank until they were out of sight and then crept along until they were level with the far end of the train.

Jack was in the lead, and he now began to crawl up the bank until he could see over the top. He beckoned the others up to him.

"This is the plan," he said. "They're all getting into the train now. We must crawl up one at a time and dash over the line and get into one of the carriages that's got a few people in it. Try and look as if you've come round the other way from the platform. Choose the carriage you're going to make for, and then go straight for it. Now—who's going first? Shall I?"

"Yes, you go first," said Betty.

"All right. Don't you follow till you see me comfortably settled. Good-bye . . . I'm off!"

Jack crawled up to the top of the bank and then ran, bent double, until he reached the train. No one saw him coming, and he climbed into a carriage just as some other boys were getting in from the platform side. That hid him perfectly from any grown-ups who might have been watching, and he now looked expectantly out towards the bank of the canal and made little signs for the others to hurry up.

Apparently there was an argument going on as to which of the Brew children should go first. Neither wanted to be left behind. In the end, when Jack was nearly frantic thinking they would miss the train, they both ran up together and got in as easily as Jack had done.

They sat very still while the train puffed its way out of the station and across the fields. It did a lot of hooting and whistling, for there were always sheep and lambs straying over the line from the fields, and sometimes there was even a cow. The first stop was at Burmarsh Halt, where an old woman with a shopping basket got in, and here Jack and his friends managed to get together in a carriage near the end of the train.

"That's fine," said Jack gaily. "Dymchurch next; then Littlestone; then Dungeness. I wonder if we shall be able to see the lighthouse."

"Someone might treat us," said Betty hopefully, but as it happened no one did. They mooned about on the shingle until the train was ready to return, and then got aboard in the last carriage again.

But this time they were not so lucky. They were shouting and hanging out of the window as they went along, and one of the grown-up passengers in the train must have complained, because at Littlestone the stationmaster came and told them to be quiet, and then asked to see their tickets.

Jack went crimson, but Betty had an answer ready.

"My mum's farther up the train, and she's got them," she said.

The stationmaster went away, and Betty began to feel very pleased with herself.

"They believe anything you tell them," she said airily. "We'll be all right now."

"I wish the train would go, though," said Jack miserably. "It didn't stand here so long on the way down. I wonder what it's waiting for?"

"Oh, don't fuss!" said Betty impatiently, but just then the stationmaster re-appeared.

"Out you get, all three of you," he said grimly. "I've asked all up the train, and nobody's ever heard of you."

They crawled out, looking very much ashamed of themselves.

"We can't walk all the way back to Hythe," wailed Betty. "It's ten miles."

"That'll teach you to steal rides on trains without a ticket, and then tell lies about it," said the stationmaster sternly. "Off you go . . . out of my sight." He gave a signal to the driver, and as the three children slunk along the road they saw their train pull out of the station and puff away through the fields.

It was a long, long walk, and they were very hot and tired and thirsty long before they reached the end of it. Jack had ample opportunity to think of what he had done, and to realize that it did not look too good for a boy who had promised to be a follower of the Lord Jesus. He began to whisper little prayers, saying he was sorry, and then another thought struck him. Was he only sorry because he had to walk home? Would he have realized that he had done wrong, and said he was sorry for it, if the train had taken them nicely back to Hythe again?

He tramped along, trying to sort out what he would or would not have done, until he was quite honestly glad that the stationmaster had found them and turned them off the train. At least he knew now that he had done wrong, and could say he was sorry for it, while if things had turned out differently he might have shut his eyes to the wrongdoing and pretended that everything was all right.

All the time Betty and Tony were grumbling and moaning and blaming each other and Jack for landing them all in this mess. At last Jack stopped thinking and noticed them.

"I don't know what you're making such a fuss about," he said. "We asked for it, and we've got it. Now we've got to put up with it."

"If Betty'd said we'd lost the tickets instead of saying Mum had got them, it would have been all right," said Tony.

"It wouldn't. It would have been a lie, and the man would still have turned us off. You've always got to pay for it if you do something wrong. Well, we knew it was wrong and so we're paying for it," said Jack.

"You didn't think we'd have to walk home, or you wouldn't have come," said Betty furiously.

"I didn't think about it at all, or I wouldn't have come," said Jack. "I'd have known it was wrong if I'd stopped to think, but I didn't. Anyway, I'm not going to whine now—I know it's all my own fault."

This point of view did not please the other two, and they continued to grumble and moan. At long last they reached home, and Jack went in to face his mother.

"Well, where on earth have you been?" she exclaimed. "You're ever so late—the tea's all cleared away."

"I pinched a ride on the baby train to Dungeness," said Jack, looking very white. "And I got turned off at Littlestone and had to walk back. I—I'm sorry, Mum."

"Sorry? I should think you are sorry," said his mother, staring at him in amazement. "Up you go to bed this instant moment—no, wash first, and then up you go. Not one drop of tea for you, my boy. And what your father will say when he comes in I don't know. I shall have to tell him."

"I know," said Jack, and went into the back kitchen to wash. He bathed his aching feet and his hot head, and then went up to bed. He was very tired, very hungry and very unhappy, and he cried a little as he lay there, thinking how sorry his father would be to hear what his son had done.

Presently Mr. Godden returned from the boat, where he had been making preparations for the night's fishing.

"Jack not in yet?" he asked as soon as he came in.

"Yes, he's in, and I've sent him up to bed without any tea. Whatever do you think he's been doing?" said Mrs. Godden, and she told her husband what Jack had told her.

Mr. Godden stood and thought for a few minutes.

"Poor little lad," he said at last. "He said he was sorry, did he?"

"Yes, he did, and I'm sure he was," said Mrs. Godden. "But to do a thing like that!"

"He won't do it again," said Ben Godden. "I think I'll go up and see him. No tea, did you say? I think I'll take him up a bit of bread and jam. I expect he's feeling pretty bad, one way and another."

Jack heard his father's footsteps on the stairs, and sat up in bed. He looked very woebegone as his father came in and sat down on the bed beside him.

"Well, son, the devil won that round, did he?" asked Mr. Godden quietly.

Jack nodded.

"Yes, Dad. Oh, Dad—how ever could I have done it? And I might never have realized how bad it was if we hadn't got turned off the train. But really I'm not sorry only because we had to walk; I'm really and truly sorry. And the worst of it is," cried Jack with a burst of tears, "that I'd promised the Lord Jesus to follow Him and fight on His side, and now He'll never believe me again!"

"Oh, yes, He will, son," said his father, holding the boy very tightly to him. "Don't you remember how badly Peter let Him down, and then went on to be one of the greatest of the apostles? Pick yourself up and start again, son. He is there to help you. He loves you, don't forget, just as I love you. He's sorry you did it, just as I'm sorry you did it, but we'll put it behind us now and forget it. He can wash away our sins, remember, and He will if you ask Him. Now cheer up and eat this bit of bread and jam I've brought up for you."

"Oh, Dad," said Jack with a sigh and a snuffle, "you are the best father that every lived!"

Chapter 13

FOG!

THE holidays were over and school had started again. All the summer visitors had left Hythe, and the beach was deserted nowadays except for the fishermen, and sometimes the Hythe children themselves. But the October gales were blustery and cold, and there was no fun on the beach in weather like that. Sometimes it was too bad for the fishing boats to go out, and the men spent their time in repairing their nets and sails, and looking after their ropes. And sometimes they stayed at home and got in the way when their wives wanted to turn out the cottage.

Some of the men, who had not put money by during the good season when they could go fishing every night, now found themselves in difficulties because they had not a good catch to sell every morning. Arthur Brew was one of these, and the shrill voice of quarrelling could sometimes be heard from their cottage as his wife complained that she could not buy food without money. Then Brew would come round and ask shamefacedly if he could borrow a little from Ben Godden, and of course he never went away empty-handed.

But Ben would not lend him money for drink.

Food, yes—but drink, no; that was his firm, last word. And so Mr. Brew was more sober and had fewer headaches during the bad season than during the good times of the summer.

Jack could not help knowing what was going on, but his father would never discuss it with him. Sometimes Mrs. Godden scolded her husband a little for pouring good money into a bottomless pit, as she called it.

"He'll never pay you back," she said. "I don't know why you do it."

"I can't see the children go hungry, and neither could you, Mum," he would say, and she would shrug her shoulders and sigh, for she knew that he was right.

"I'll tell you another reason," said Ben Godden. "Whoso giveth to the poor, lendeth to the Lord. You know that, don't you?"

"But it's his own fault he's poor," protested Mrs. Godden. "If he didn't drink so much he wouldn't have to borrow. He doesn't deserve that you should help him."

"Perhaps he doesn't, but do we *deserve* that the Lord Jesus should have come down from Heaven and died on the cross for us? Was it because we deserved it, or because He loved us, that he came?"

"We don't deserve it, that's certain," sighed Mrs. Godden. "No, it was love . . . and I know what you mean. St. John says, 'If God so loved us, we ought also to love one another.' But how you can love a good-for-nothing like Arthur Brew beats me."

"God loves him, and the bells will ring in heaven on the day that he's converted," said Ben Godden. "Now here's a funny thing about you," he went on teasingly to his wife, "you'll give money to help black savages that you've never seen, but you grudge help to the man who lives next door. Are you going to tell me that a wild savage living in a forest is better worth converting than poor old Arthur?"

"No, of course not," said Mrs. Godden, laughing. "But we've got to think of the savages too."

"Yes, that's right, and I'd be the last to grudge a penny spent in that way. They're God's children too, but don't let all your love and charity be for the black man and none for the white. Do the thing that's nearest, is a pretty good motto, to my way of thinking. I'm going to hammer away at old Arthur until, by God's mercy, he's converted. And I shan't do much good if I pull a long face and refuse to help him when he's really in need."

"It wouldn't do for everybody to think only of the man next door," argued Mrs. Godden. "There'd be no missions to foreign places if we all did that."

"You're right again," said her husband, "but what it boils down to is this . . . God puts into your heart what He wants you to do. Some He calls out to be missionaries, and some teachers and preachers, and some just ordinary humble fishermen like myself . . ."

"But you can all be fishers of men," put in

Jack suddenly, remembering what the missioner had said in the summer.

"I didn't know you were listening, son, but you're right," said his father with a smile. "Whatever our job, we can be fishers of men."

Jack sometimes reflected that it was a funny thing that his mother should have protested against his father helping the Brews, because she always put a little parcel for them into Jack's overcoat pocket with his own lunch. It would be either a slice of cake each, or a bun, or just a slice of bread and dripping. They had school milk, of course, and school dinners, but she did not like to think of them with nothing to eat when they went out for break in the middle of the morning.

Jack thought a good bit from time to time about what his father had said with regard to Mr. Brew, and it seemed to him that if he could do something of the same sort with Tony and Betty it would be a grand thing. He did not quite know how to set about it, though, and so, after pondering for a while, he asked his father.

"Dad, how do you get people converted?"

"Prayer first of all," was the prompt reply, "then example, and finally a word now and again . . . but no preaching unless you're a preacher and it's your job."

"Oh," said Jack, thoughtfully.

"What's in your mind, son?" asked his father.

"I want to be a fisher of men too," explained Jack.

"Well, that's fine. First you pray to the Lord

Jesus about the person you have in mind; and not only once or twice, but pray regularly. Keep it up. Don't let yourself get slack. Morning and evening, and any other time you set aside to talk to your Heavenly Father, remember them before Him and pray that the Holy Spirit may work in their hearts. That's the first step, and the easiest. The second one is hard, and that's to let them see by your behaviour that belonging to the Lord is something worth while. Let them see that it means something to you. Let them see that being a Christian is a happy thing, and a brave thing. Make them interested, so that they want to know more about it."

"That's not easy when you've known them all your life," said Jack.

"No, it isn't easy—I told you that. And the third thing is the most difficult of all, perhaps. You've got to be ready with the right word to help them at the right time. Don't argue with them, and don't nag them or you'll make them sick of the subject. But always be on the look-out to say a word for the Lord."

"I see," said Jack. "I'm glad you don't think I ought to preach to them, because I don't see how I could do it. They wouldn't listen to me."

"I don't suppose they would," agreed his father. "But the most important part of the whole thing is prayer. God alone can convert anyone, by the power of His Holy Spirit, but He does use us to help sometimes. So concentrate on prayer."

Jack made up his mind to do this, and he very rarely forgot to include Tony and Betty in his prayers after that. As for the other things his father had said, sometimes he remembered them and sometimes he didn't, but he honestly tried. But for some time Tony and Betty seemed to be no different in spite of the efforts being made on their behalf.

Jack took this puzzle to his father one rough November evening.

"Dad, I've been praying and doing all the things you said, but God isn't doing anything about it. They're just the same."

"How do you know what He's doing?" asked Ben Godden with a twinkle in his eye. "The Holy Spirit is working in their hearts, preparing the ground. You go on doing your side of it, and He'll go on doing His."

"Well, it takes an awful long time," sighed Jack.

"How long do you suppose I've been praying for Mr. Brew?" asked his father quietly.

Jack was silent for a moment.

"Don't you get tired of it?" he asked presently.

"No," said Mr. Godden slowly. "I don't get tired of it exactly. I know it's likely to be a long job; I know I may probably never see the end of it until I meet Arthur Brew in heaven. But I'm content to go on in faith. Don't lose faith, son. Keep pegging away."

Jack was surprised one day when Mr. Emsworth stopped him in the road.

"I notice your young friends the Brews are coming along to Sunday School a bit more regularly," he said. "I expect that's your doing, isn't it?"

"I . . . er . . . yes, I suppose it is," admitted Jack.

"Good for you. Keep at it," said the curate, and would have passed on but Jack remembered he had something to tell him.

"I wanted to tell you something," he said rather gruffly, because he was feeling shy.

"What is it?" asked the curate with a smile, thinking it was probably another scrape of some sort. "Out with it!"

"The man who was here with the mission in the summer said I ought to tell you," said Jack. " At least, he said you'd like to know."

Mr. Emsworth began to look keenly interested.

"That sounds as though it's something important," he said.

"Well, it's important to me," said Jack. "I don't suppose you'd think it frightfully important, really. It's just that . . . well, you said once . . . at least, you've said it lots of times, but . . . well, you said something about making up our minds to follow the Lord Jesus and fight on His side for the rest of our lives. And . . . well . . . I've done it, that's all."

"But that's grand!" said Mr. Emsworth, holding out his hand. "That's simply magnificent. I'm tremendously glad, Jack. Shake hands! You'll find it's a hard life, but it's a man's life, and worth it all the way. Now look here, if there's ever anything you want to know, and want help about, in any way at all, come and see me, won't you? I expect your father could help you better than I could, really . . . I know him, and he's one of the best men I know . . . but come to me any time you like. We're fellow-soldiers for Christ now, and anything I can do for you, I will."

"Thank you, sir," said Jack.

"That's cheered me up for a week," said Mr. Emsworth, and they both laughed as they parted again.

The weather seemed better for a day or two after this, and the fishing boats began to go out again. But there came a night when Jack woke up suddenly with a feeling that something was wrong. The boats were out, and both Jack and his mother were liable to wake up if there was any change in the weather, but although he now listened for rising wind or rain, there was nothing to be heard at all.

Nothing at first, but then a strange sound, a sound full of foreboding to those who live by the sea, came across the waves towards them. A moaning sound, ending with a rough grunt. Jack knew what it was—the Dungeness fog-horn, sending out its message of danger to all within earshot.

He got out of bed and went to the window, drawing aside the curtains by the light of his pocket torch. He could see nothing; everything was blank and dark outside. He opened the window, and then it swirled in . . . thick, yellow fog, clammy and cold, like wisps of yellow smoke in the light of the torch. Jack closed the window again, and went to see if his mother was awake.

Chapter 14

FISHERS OF MEN

A CANDLE was burning on the table by Mrs. Godden's bed when Jack went in, but she was kneeling by the window.

"Are you awake, Mum?" he asked.

She turned at once.

"Come in, dear. Yes, I couldn't sleep with that row going on. Was that what woke you too?"

"The old fog-horn, yes," said Jack. He went over and stood beside his mother. "Do you think they're all right? What's the time, Mum?"

"A quarter past four," she said with a shiver.

"They ought to have been in before now," said Jack.

"Perhaps they've anchored. That's what they'd do, for sure. They wouldn't try to get in with this fog . . . they couldn't see a hand held in front of their faces. They'll have anchored till it blows over."

"It might last for days," said Jack in a troubled voice.

"They'll be hungry if it does," said Mrs. Godden, trying to laugh. "No it won't last for days, dear. It'll go when the tide turns, I dare say."

"I hate the sound of that old fog-horn," muttered Jack.

"So do I," said his mother. "Yet we ought to be thankful for it. It's saved thousands of lives. But it always means trouble, and even when your dad's at home, I can't help thinking of the men out there when it goes off."

"I wonder if Tony and Betty are awake," said Jack.

"Poor Mrs. Brew—it's worse for her," said Mrs. Godden. "I think I ought to go in and see if she's all right." She got up and began to put a heavy coat on over her dressing-gown.

"Can I come too, Mum?" asked Jack.

"Yes. Put your socks and boots on, and your big coat. We'll see if there are any lights on in the cottage, and if there are we'll go in."

There was a light in the kitchen of the next-door cottage, and Mrs. Godden knocked and went in. Mrs. Brew was sitting by the dying embers of a fire, crying quietly to herself, while the two children huddled in a chair on the opposite side of the hearth.

"I thought you might have heard it," said Mrs. Godden. "We couldn't sleep either."

"I shall never see him again," moaned Mrs. Brew, and the two children howled at the words.

"Come, come—don't take it like that," said Mrs. Godden. "They'll cast anchor and lie there till the wind rises and takes the fog away. Don't lose heart."

"A great steamer will come and run them down," moaned Mrs. Brew. "That's what happens in a fog."

Mrs. Godden sighed and did not answer for a

moment. She knew the danger that little ships run in such weather conditions, when bigger ships may find themselves off their course, and terrible accidents may occur in a moment. Such things had happened, she knew well, and for the moment she could not find an answer to the other woman's words.

"God won't let that happen," said Jack, surprised that his mother was silent.

"I don't suppose He concerns Himself about it at all," said Mrs. Brew, snuffling. "He doesn't bother His head about poor people like us."

"Come now, you know that isn't true," said Mrs. Godden. "He cares for each one of us, or why should He have come down from heaven to die for us? Look here—let me put a kettle on and rake the fire together a bit. We shan't sleep, either of us, with our men out there. We could have a bit of a talk."

"Just as you like," said Mrs. Brew.

"You children go back to bed," said Mrs. Godden, taking charge of the situation. "Jack can go in with Tony if he likes. Go on . . . you'll catch your death of cold down here."

So the three children went upstairs, and Jack got in with Tony while Betty went into her own small bedroom, leaving the door open, so that they could talk. For a little while the talk was all about shipwrecks and dreadful things like that.

"Do you remember that hymn we had in Sunday School last week?" asked Jack suddenly. " 'For those in peril on the sea.' Let's sing it."

"I don't know it very well," said Tony doubtfully.

"Never mind; join in when you can," said Jack, and so they sang it, and when they came to the lines, "Oh, hear us when we cry to Thee, For those in peril on the sea," Tony joined in.

"Do you think that does any good?" asked Betty, coming in wrapped in a coat.

"Yes, I do," said Jack. "It's like singing a prayer, and God always answers prayers."

"Do you mean that if I prayed for a million pounds, God would send it?" asked Tony scornfully.

"No, it isn't like that," said Jack. "It has to be a proper prayer, not a selfish one. But He *does* answer prayers if He knows you love Him. It isn't much good praying to Him just when you want something, and not thinking about Him at all any other time."

"How can you love Him?" asked Betty. "You've never seen Him."

"No, but I've heard about Him, and I know what He did for me," said Jack. "And, somehow, if you make up your mind to follow Him and fight on His side, you get to love Him more and more. The more you know about Him, and the more you talk to Him and try to please Him, the more you find yourself loving Him. I've found that out."

"Did you promise to follow Him and fight on His side?" asked Tony curiously.

"Yes," said Jack.

"Why?" asked Betty.

"Because He died for me, to save me from the devil," said Jack. "And I'm going to fight for Him all my life. You've got to choose some time or another, you know, whether you'll fight on the Lord's side or on the devil's. And I'm going to fight on the Lord's."

"But I couldn't be good *all* the time," said Tony fretfully. "Would the devil get me if I wasn't good all the time?"

"Not if you really love the Lord Jesus and are trying to follow Him," said Jack. "The devil can't touch you then. But if you're only pretending, he'll get you all right."

"*You're* not always good," said Betty. "I thought you'd have to be terribly good if you promised to follow the Lord Jesus. I'm sure I couldn't do it."

"If you promise to follow Him, Jesus helps you to be good," said Jack. "And He forgives us when we go wrong, if we're really sorry. I—I do wish you would follow Him. I've been praying for ever such a long time that you would."

"You've been praying for us?" asked Betty in astonishment.

"That's cheek," said Tony.

"No, it isn't; it's because you're my friends, and I wanted you to be on the same side too. I wanted you to get to know the Lord Jesus, as I'm beginning to know Him. I do wish you would. He loves you, you know."

"Why should He love us?" asked Betty.

"I don't know *why* He does, but He does," said

Jack. "If you'd really get to know Him, you'd realize that too."

"All right," said Betty suddenly. "I will. What do I have to do?"

"Just tell Him that you want to follow Him and fight for Him, and ask Him to help you to do it properly," said Jack.

Betty knelt down.

"Wait . . . I'm going to, too," said Tony, and scrambled down beside her. Jack got out too and knelt down, but he prayed quietly, and thanked the Lord Jesus for answering his prayer about his friends, and asked the Lord to help them and to show them what to do. Then they all got back into their beds again, and were soon asleep.

When they woke up the fog had cleared, and a crisp, bright sun was shining. They all dressed quickly, and went downstairs, where they found the two mothers asleep in front of the fire. Jack put the kettle on and was just making a pot of tea when his mother woke up.

"Oh . . . did I go to sleep?" she said in surprise.

"Looks like it," said Jack. "The fog's cleared and the sun's shining. Let's go down to the beach and see if we can see the *Mary Uden*, shall we?"

"I'll run in home and dress," said Mrs. Godden. "You make a cup of tea, there's a good boy, but don't wake Mrs. Brew unless she stirs. I shan't be two ticks."

She was very quickly back, and Mrs. Brew woke up, and they all had a hot drink and some bread and jam before putting on their thickest coats and going down to the beach. The three children ran on ahead, and when Betty—who was the fastest because she had the longest legs—reached the road that runs along the edge of the shingle, she gave a great shout.

"They're coming in!"

How the two women hurried up then! Yes, there was the boat, sailing in as though nothing had happened. They ran down to the water's edge to help it in, and the two men waved and shouted as they saw their families waiting for them.

When they had jumped ashore and drawn the boat up away from the waves, Mr. Godden turned to his wife with a smile.

"You had an anxious night—but it's all turned out for the best, as you'll agree when you hear the news."

"Wait till you hear *my* news," cried Mrs. Godden. "It's Mrs. Brew's news really. We had ever such a long talk last night, and . . ."

"And . . . and I've given my heart to the Lord at last," said Mrs. Brew nervously. "And I hope He helps me to be a better woman."

"Have you done it too, love?" asked Arthur Brew, coming forward and taking his wife's hand. "Well, I am glad of that, for Ben Godden's had his way at last, and I've taken the plunge too. I'm a converted man, my dear, and I hope you'll see a difference in me from now on."

Well, what a joyful reunion that was, with everyone shaking hands with everyone else. Betty and Tony stood aside at first, staring at their parents, until Tony touched Jack on the arm.

"Does that mean they've done what we did last night?"

"Yes, that's right," said Jack.

Tony gave a whoop of delight, and ran up to his father and grabbed his hand.

"Dad—I've done it too, and so's Betty. We're all on the same side now!"

"All on the Lord's side," said Ben Godden. "Praise be to God."